THE OX-FILES

The Ox-Files

WEIRD & WONDERFUL TALES OF OXFORDSHIRE

[signature]

Mike White

*This is dedicated to Peter White
who brought us all to this amazing county.
Thanks for everything Dad.*

First published in 2023

by Palatine Books
Carnegie House
Chatsworth Road
Lancaster LA1 4SL
www.palatinebooks.com

Copyright © Mike White

All rights reserved
Unauthorised duplication contravenes existing laws

The right of Mike White to be identified as the author of this work has been asserted in accordance with the Copyright, Designs and Patents act 1988

British Library Cataloguing-in-Publication data
A catalogue record for this book is available from the British Library

Every effort has been made to trace copyright holders.

Paperback isbn 13: 978-1-910837-46-7

Designed and typeset by Carnegie Book Production
www.carnegiebookproduction.com

Printed and bound by Ashford

Contents

Introduction	vii
Out and About	1
A Certain Lack of Patients	13
Not Exactly a Barrel of Laughs	17
Beastly Behaviour	25
Not Just Any Tom, Dick and Harry	31
Oxfordshire Rocks	37
A Relatively Haunted Hotel	49
Featuring Creatures	53
RiOtmoor	61
Serving Spirits	67
Oxford's Most Haunted College	79
Witches, Wizards and Wise Folk	85
Pond Memories	95
Notes from a Lady	105
A Vacation Visitation	109
The Students are Revolting	113
Unearthly De-lights	117
Haunted People	123
A Parson Investigates	129
A Triad of Tragedies	137
Felix Aviatrix	147
The Bicester Warlock	151
Tales from the Riverbank	155
The North Aston Terror	163
King Alfred's Head and Tales	171
Things That Go Bump in the Night	179
Epilogue	183

Introduction

While Oxford is justifiably famous for its history (and its ghost stories of course) the county of Oxfordshire is far more than just the eponymous city and can boast a fascinating and varied range of stories of its own – as I hope to show. From Faringdon to Banbury, Henley to the edge of the Cotswolds, and not forgetting Oxford itself of course, I have tried to cover a diverse range of topics in this book: standing stones that do more than stand; witches and cunning folk, both cursing and curing; odd and out-of-place animals (including a genuinely odd cat); highwaymen and other ne'er-do-wells; eerie lights in the skies; riotous behaviour of various sorts; and, of course, a plethora of ghost stories.

I have avoided a simple geographical survey of the county, aiming for a more thematic, if slightly scattergun, approach. There are some stories from a particular location or based on individual witness accounts but some sections are loosely arranged around various themes to highlight similarities and differences in the way the accounts are related. And possibly to highlight the sheer variety of some of these tales …. A few of these narratives may be well-known but many have been told to me personally by witnesses or correspondents, some have been unearthed from local press* or historical archives and one or two come direct from my own investigations. From the Civil War to the present-day people have been witnessing the weird and wonderful across the county – I hope you enjoy reading their stories.

---

* Including the *Oxford Mail* which, I discover, ran a column called the Ox-Files for a brief period in the 1990s. Kudos to them for stealing my title *from the future*. There's our first mystery right there.

The track from Hanborough to Freeland

Out and About

SOMETIMES I WONDER WHETHER it is possible to step outside the door in Oxfordshire without running into something slightly supernatural. If you should be out and about, please keep your eyes open for one of the many mysterious migrant manifestations which haunt our highways and byways. For example ...

There is said to be a phantom coach which drives up the road from North Leigh to Freeland. Late one night and many years ago a young man was riding his bicycle from Freeland towards Oxford when, as he coasted down the hill out of the village, he heard the sound of someone galloping towards him. Concerned that whatever was coming would be unable to see him, he got off his bike and pulled it over to the side of the highway. Almost immediately there was a rumbling and a clattering and something passed by him on the road, invisible but accompanied by the unmistakable sound of horses' hooves upon the ground. Although he had not been able to see anything at all he, not unnaturally perhaps, assumed the noise had been that of a ghostly carriage and horses abroad on some mysterious eldritch errand.

This non-apparition had already made another non-appearance some years earlier. A couple riding a wagon loaded with corn were driving down the same road when the husband similarly heard something racing towards them from behind. He hastily pulled his horses to the side of the road to let it pass, but as he did so his wife turned to him asking, 'What-ever are you doing that for?' She had heard nothing of the encounter nor seen anything and was, to say the least, surprised when he described hearing a coach and horses gallop by. The same coach was heard on another occasion by a woman living at the bottom of the same hill. She was walking upwards with a friend, when they too heard a carriage approaching. They pressed themselves against the wall at the roadside, and heard it pass quite near, rattling by at a full gallop down the hill, but again, saw nothing at all.

Luckily, most phantom coaches are rather more willing to put in a proper appearance. There is a pond in Eynsham which dries out during particularly warm weather and on these occasions a phantom coach trapped within it is freed to drive around the village. Local legend has it that the driver is a particularly nasty previous inhabitant of Eynsham Hall but I have no further details I'm afraid. In another random snippet of a tale a Mr. B. described how, when he was a young boy and delivering bread near Chadlington, he had rounded a corner in his wagon only to discover a coach and horses straddling the path ahead of him. Unable to stop in time he was simultaneously terrified and relieved when he passed completely through the phantom carriage, shaken and most definitely stirred. At least this apparition had the decency to stay outside; a ghostly carriage once observed by a certain Mrs Beachcroft drove right inside Water Eaton House before disappearing.

Another phantom coach used to be a feature of Wardington Manor, which was owned by George Chamberlayne in the time of Charles II.[*] In Chamberlayne's will he specified that he should be buried in Wardington churchyard, but his wife ignored his stated wishes and arranged for him to be interred with members of her family at Hillesden in Buckinghamshire. Chamberlayne was clearly not a spirit to take this lying down and took to driving his horses and carriage round the Manor House each night, causing much disruption until his family finally relented and had his body laid to rest as his will required. After achieving this post-mortem objective, he retired to his grave forever.

There is an (unspecified) anniversary sighting of a tragic collision at the crossroads in the village of Rowstock. At least we have a back story here, although the tale is a sorry one. In the winter of

---

[*] To make this clear he had his initials and the date 1666 carved into the lead pipework of the building.

1709, a young junior army officer was eloping with his sweetheart, taking the coach from Newbury to marry in secret, far from their presumably disapproving families. Unfortunately, as their coach reached the crossroads it ran headlong into the Gloucester mail coach heading towards London. After the devastating crash, in which both vehicles were destroyed, the dead bodies of the young sweethearts were pulled from the wreckage by horrified rescuers. I am not aware of anyone who has actually been witness to this awful apparition nor, unfortunately, of the actual date of the crash so this is likely to be a long, cold investigation should anyone be of a mind to confirm the story.

There is another similar tale from the Stert crossroads at Sydenham which also suffered a stagecoach accident – although in this case the coach overturned at speed, killing its occupants. Rather than manifesting as a ghostly apparition it seems that the malign effects of the accident have left a psychic stain or patch of paranormal pollution to haunt the area which has become something of a notorious accident black spot ever since. Sydenham seems to have an affinity for what writer T. C. Lethbridge called 'ghouls', the unpleasant residue of some past emotional trauma, because walkers along Sewell's Lane (a track linking the village with the Lower Icknield Way) have also reported experiencing 'a cold, ghostly feeling' on this isolated pathway.

And next, a rather more dramatic, and thankfully less anonymous, apparition. Sir George Cobb of Adderbury died at the impressive age of 90 when he fell into a pond whilst visiting one of his daughters at Reading in 1762. In his will he directed that four beautiful oak trees in his grounds were to be left untouched but, for some reason, after his death his wishes were ignored and the trees were felled. You may not be surprised to discover that his ghost soon began to be observed at the spot the trees had occupied. One evening two men were poaching in a nearby stream and saw Sir George's coach and four coming towards them, the horses breathing fire. Terrified (as well they might be) they fled – and were so shocked that they resolved never to poach again.

And if you think that was a terrifying encounter spare a thought for travellers along the turnpike road past Witney. Part of this stretch, just beside an area called Ousen Bottom, was the haunt of 'a little man in black silk stockings who always carries his head under his arm' who was in the habit of running alongside passing carriages and would sometimes even climb up alongside the driver, doubtless to the consternation of all concerned. Apparently, according to Angelina Parker writing in *Folklore*, 'the passengers were very much alarmed when this first happened, but after a time they got used to it and did not mind him in the least'. Should you happen to spot this apparition as you cruise past Witney on the A40 I trust you will show equal aplomb.

Obviously, a ghost doesn't always need a carriage. After a farmer named Faulkner died near Drayton St. Leonard in the mid-nineteenth century his spirit was frequently seen riding his favourite horse along the lanes and across the fields of his old farm. One old man named Hicks remembered how while out walking with his uncle shortly after Faulkner's transition to ectoplasmic equestrian, they had noticed a rider coming across a field towards a gate. Being helpful folk, they naturally rushed to open the gate for the horseman, only to watch with a mixture of fascination and horror as both horse and rider passed un-noticing through the gate before they had chance to reach it.

There are also stories of encounters with ghostly horses on the road from Steventon to East Hanney, the most well-known being a report from a young woman who described a number of insubstantial grey animals drifting across the road in front of her car. These apparitions then leapt over the hedge by the roadside and disappeared. A driver and passenger who were travelling from Steventon into Hanney in 2006 experienced something similar, in this case a lone horse which galloped from a side road and out in front of their vehicle. They turned off their headlights briefly to avoid panicking what they assumed to be an escaped animal, but when they switched them back on it was just in time to watch the apparition vanish before their eyes. The field beside which this sighting happened is chillingly called Deadman's Ham.

Better than a simple ghost rider, Abingdon can boast a mounted mountebank who rides through Bagley Wood on especially dark nights. This mysterious figure is never identified but is assumed to be a highwayman because he follows an old path hidden deep within the darkest and most inaccessible part of the woods. The ground level was evidently lower during his lifetime as his ghost, or rather that of his horse, seems to be walking on a path some distance below the surface of the ground today.

There are reports of ghosts using more modern forms of transport of course. Hook Norton supposedly has a ghostly cyclist who has been seen coming down the hill towards Traitor's Ford and then disappearing before he completes his journey. It has been speculated that this spectral cyclist might be Alban Clarke, a senior manager of the Hook Norton Brewery at the time the present building was constructed, who borrowed a bicycle one afternoon with the intention of going fishing in Traitor's Ford Brook in May 1917 but lost control, crashed and later died of his injuries.

I have a couple of other examples of psychical cyclists. A couple walking through Hinksey Park in 2017 reported watching as a man on a bike rode along a path and passed behind a tree, never to reappear, but a rather more terrifying apparition has been seen on Magdalen Bridge. Back in the 1960s an un-named

Magdalen Bridge; no sign of a pate-less peddler here

woman and her daughter, Jane, who were driving across the bridge one misty November evening approached a tweed-clad cyclist on what they described as an old and rickety bike. As they pulled out to overtake both women were horrified to realise that he was entirely headless.* They looked at each other in amazement, shocked at what they had seen, and agreed never to discuss their ghostly encounter with anyone else for fear of being ridiculed. Until, that is, Jane heard the story of a cyclist who was hit by a car in the 1930s and tragically killed on the spot. Learning that he had been decapitated in the accident, she shared the story with the *Oxford Mail* hoping to hear from someone else who had encountered the apparition. Sadly, she had no luck in unearthing any other witnesses so this seems to have been a one-off sighting, but it does make me wonder whether a headless cyclist would be the modern equivalent of the headless horseman of times past?**

The college grounds below Magdalen Bridge in which the featureless phantom figures

Coincidentally, a misty figure has also been observed walking in the college grounds below the bridge. When this figure approached a man out walking one evening, he was terrified to discover that its facial features were entirely absent and immediately turned and fled. It would be interesting to know if there is any connection between these two apparitions.

Some ghosts seem to be content to take the air, or whatever

---

* How they had failed to spot this earlier is not explained. Perhaps they thought he was simply hunched forwards?
** Severed cyclist? Beheaded bicyclist? Vertically-truncated velocipedist? Catchy terminology is more difficult to coin than you might think.

passes for air on the other side, in a more relaxed fashion. After Sir Christopher Willoughby, Squire of Marsh Baldon, died in 1808 he was buried with all due ceremony in the village churchyard and life in the village moved on. But not entirely without him. His restless spirit took to strolling around the lanes of the village at dusk, much to the consternation of those he encountered. He was particularly fond of Daglen Lane, the road to Nuneham Courtenay, where he was often seen by village residents, sauntering along with his hands deep in the pockets of his favourite brown coat, easily recognisable because of its bright metal buttons. Although he seemed totally harmless his continuing presence was deemed too unsettling for comfort and his ghost was eventually laid to rest in Baldon Manor library.[*]

Here is a story from the late 1990s.[**] Matt was walking home to Stanton St John after a night out in Forest Hill one evening in late summer. The air was warm and a nearly full moon meant that the night was well lit and 'almost as bright as day'. Given that it was rather late at night Matt was surprised to see a tall figure approaching him; he was even more surprised to see that the figure, when it came closer, was a man dressed in a long black coat and wearing a tall black hat. Matt stepped aside to let the gentleman pass and then moved onwards but, on a whim, turned back around to study the curious figure, only to discover that he was nowhere to be seen. The hedge beside the footpath had been trimmed to a height of around 1.5 metres (4–5ft) so the figure could, in theory, have climbed over and hidden but, given the way he was dressed and the total lack of any sound to indicate that he had scrambled over the hedge, this seemed unlikely.

The combination of the old-fashioned figure's clothes and unexplained disappearance suddenly filled Matt with a sense of panic and he sprinted home as fast as he could. Falling through the front door, breathless and shaking, he started to stammer out an explanation of his experience to his mother. Before he had the chance to do so she held up her hand. 'You have just seen the ghost haven't you?' she asked, adding that she and

---
[*] Does this mean that the library is now full of exorcise books?
[**] A number of the following stories come from an old correspondent, HMY in Wheatley. I'm glad to finally be able to bring them to light.

The road from Stanton St John to Forest Hill

Matt's father had seen the same man at the same spot on the road over forty years earlier.

I am not aware of any other sightings of the figure but it has been suggested that the strangely-garbed gentleman is John White, one-time Warden of New College, puritan preacher and one of the Founding Fathers of the US state of Massachusetts, who was born in Stanton St John in 1575. Now, obviously, this is a somewhat dubious conclusion but, having no other suggestions to offer, if the tall, black puritan hat fits ...

Sometimes people encounter rather more formless phantoms. For example, a stile in the fields behind Mill Lane in Old Marston is haunted by an amorphous apparition, a misty manifestation which has been observed on a number of occasions by walkers in the area. Apparently, it appears as a swirling cloud radiating cold and hovering some way above the ground. Thankfully, this is nowhere near as terrifying as the black cloud which has been reported from the roads outside Burford. In this case drivers passing through it are overcome by unaccountable feelings of utter terror and animals which wander nearby are panicked into flight.

No terrifying clouds here, but there is a stretch of road between Chinnor and Aston Rowant which has been described as having a sinister atmosphere, even by day. By night it seems to offer more tangible terrors as Sam discovered while riding his motorbike along the route one moonless night. As he passed along a stretch overhung by large, broad-leafed trees he was suddenly aware of an unnerving feeling that someone had joined him on the bike and was behind him in the pillion position. He couldn't feel any spectral arms around him, nor did he feel anything pressing up against his back, but the feeling grew nonetheless. Sam quickly accelerated away and the sense of another presence was gradually left behind.

Some weeks later he was in a car with his mother driving along the same stretch of road and, as they reached the very same spot, they became aware of a figure, illuminated by the headlight beams, walking alongside and then, suddenly, across the road. Sam described the figure as 'an old woman wrapped in a shawl, her shoulders stooped with age' although he observed that she did not so much walk as 'flitted across the road, rather like a shadow'. Both witnesses were entirely sober and looked at each other in astonishment, unable and unwilling to believe what they had just seen. Sam did attempt to find some kind of explanation behind his odd experiences and a local man told him that part of the road crossed what he called a 'witches' line' – which he defined as being the boundary between the territories of two rival witches. I did wonder if this was a misinterpretation of a ley line but there are no obvious straight-line alignments in the area to make this at all likely. Another mystery to add to our rapidly growing list.

I was tempted to put this next story in the mystery animals section* but I think that, under the circumstances, it should stand as more of a navigational hazard. Long before the construction of the current A34, Mr and Mrs Hall were driving along the old, far more rural, route between Newbury and Oxford late one evening when they decided to take a detour

---

* Coming up soon ...

and visit a friend who lived in a village just off the main road. It had clearly been a while since their last visit and after driving down a small country lane for some minutes Mr Hall began to wonder whether they had taken a wrong turning. Their view of the countryside was not helped by the torrential rain that was falling that evening and as they crawled along the rapidly-worsening road they noticed something odd in the lane up ahead of them. Both the Halls agreed that it resembled a cow as seen from the back end but what made it frightening was that it was surrounded by a nimbus of eerie, but very bright, light. Suddenly struck by the strangeness of the apparition Mr Hall decided that retreat was the most prudent option, somehow managed to turn the car around, and the couple sped back to the main road and the safety of home.

They told this story to researcher John Richardson, who revealed that he had heard a similar story from elsewhere in the county but, frustratingly, he doesn't specify where.* All we can really say is that the lesson to be learned from the Halls is that on wet nights in south Oxfordshire it's a good idea to avoid unknown side roads or you may find yourself well and truly cowed by what you encounter.

As if luminous liminal livestock weren't enough, it seems like the Devil himself has a certain fondness for parts of the county. He was said to walk Cheney Lane in Headington rattling (for some reason) a set of chains – hence (supposedly) the name of the road. He seems to have taken a particular interest in the good folk of North Leigh; on one, doubtless memorable, occasion he appeared to a group of men playing cricket on a Sunday, asked to be allowed to bowl and dismissed an entire side in short order before disappearing in a puff of, presumably sulphurous, smoke. Similarly, he once joined a group of young men out badger hunting on the Sabbath. Shouting loudly at his success he passed a sack containing a squirming animal to the group and then went on his way. When the boys opened the bag they found it contained nothing but the stink of brimstone.

'Old Nick' also appeared to a man on the road to Barnard's

---

* I can't complain, I have an unidentified location story coming up later too.

Gate, although on this occasion he assumed the form of a fiery serpent, encircling the man and trapping him for quite some time. When the unfortunate fellow was finally released he ran back to the village and brought several friends to the spot where the serpent had appeared, only to find that all evidence of the encounter had vanished.

And finally in this section, a warning should you happen to be returning from an evening out in Headington and should your path take you down Larkins or Barton Lanes. A number of revellers doing just this have found themselves accompanied by a large, and (given its saucer-sized eyes) distinctly unnatural, black dog when they have made the same trip. This was also the favoured route of an unknown man who was in the habit of taking the late-night air with his head tucked firmly under his arm. Some reports describe this apparition as a woman although that may, of course be a very different ghost. You meet all sorts in Headington. If you are really unlucky ...

The old Radcliffe Infirmary

A Certain Lack of Patients

WHEN THE RENOWNED OXFORD PHYSICIAN and politician John Radcliffe died in 1714 he left £4,000 in his will to build a hospital in Oxford on a five-acre site donated by Thomas Rowney, the MP for the city, in the area which is now St Giles.* The original Infirmary boasted five physicians and four surgeons but it gradually increased in both size and reputation over the years before finally closing as a hospital in 2007. The university purchased the building and it is now known as the Radcliffe Humanities building.**

Obviously, so many years of treating the sick and dying must have left something of a mark on the building and, indeed, any number of staff working at the hospital over the years have reported odd experiences during their time there.

Take the testimony of Susan Allmond, from Wallingford who encountered a phantom woman in the hospital as a child: 'I remember seeing a woman in an old nurse's uniform. I remember thinking she just didn't look of this time or part of the same system as everyone else. She had a pure white hat on and a different coloured belt. There was also an old woman who I saw. She was incredibly old, but she had a lovely smile. There was something different about them. You could almost see through them, and then they'd be gone.'

---

* Radcliffe had previous form in this area having already funded the Radcliffe Science Library – later housed in the Radcliffe Camera at the Bodleian Library. His will also bequeathed money to University College which has a Radcliffe Quad as a consequence.
** So that's another one to add to his list.

The latter apparition became known to staff as the 'grey lady'; perhaps Jenny Holloway's story helps explain that. Mrs Holloway worked at the RI and also encountered the spirit. 'I had a friend who used to say she'd see a little grey lady about the hospital. A lot of people laughed but I didn't. It gives me goosebumps thinking about it.'

It seems that the ghost did not restrict her appearances to within the building. Patient Adrian Taylor described his own encounter with the apparition. 'I was woken up at 2.15am by a bright light shining through my window. It was almost like sunshine. Then I heard a loud bump. I looked outside and saw a woman in an old-fashioned nurse's outfit gliding across the quadrangle down below. It was very strange' he added. Quite.

It wasn't just the staff who had a tendency to make spectral reappearances at the hospital either. Sheila Farrell, a former night nurse on the plastic surgery ward described falling asleep one night only to be woken by the feeling of a small hand stroking her cheek. Opening her eyes she saw that the help alarm for one of the ward patients was blinking redly at her (the buzzer which would accompany the alarms was disabled at night to avoid disturbing the other patients). Sheila went to answer the alarm and admitted to the man who had called her that she had only woken up because of the unknown touch. 'Oh, that'll be the children,' he replied, 'I often see them in here playing. They come and see if we're all right'. The plastic surgery unit had been the children's ward until a few years before the incident.

Other ghosts of the old building seem equally comforting. After several nights of having an unseen presence bump against his bed and constantly feeling as if 'someone was there', one patient mentioned this to his carers who confirmed that others had experienced similar phenomena. Some witnesses reported seeing the figure of a nurse who had worked at the hospital before her own death sitting beside the beds of terminally ill patients: whether she was there to offer comfort, to act as a guide to the dying person's spirit or simply as a harbinger of death is unknown. Presumably these different nurses were all different aspects of the same nocturnal Nightingale. Some observers noted that the atmosphere seemed particularly chill after her appearances. Make of that what you will.

Even now that the functions of the hospital have moved to Headington there are still occasional observations of unusual visitors in its repurposed spaces. Sue, who worked as an administrator for one of the university departments for a number of years, told me that she was passing one of the small meeting rooms in the building when she realised that there was a woman standing in the corner, even though the room was supposed to be un-booked and locked; she could not give me a description because the figure was facing away from the door but, on closer inspection, Sue realised that the figure seemed to be wearing an old-fashioned nurse's uniform. Curious as to what the woman could possibly be doing in the room, she opened the door to speak to her; in the brief moment between Sue glancing down at the door handle and entering the room the figure simply disappeared.

The bridge over the River Windrush in Burford, where Lady Tanfield's ghost lies in a bottle under the third arch

Not Exactly a Barrel of Laughs

Sir Francis Page was born in Bloxham in 1661, a younger son of the local vicar. From such humble beginnings he went on to become a lawyer and MP; he became King's Serjeant in 1715 and was eventually made Baron of the Exchequer in 1718 before being knighted in 1727, by which time he had already bought the manor of Middle Aston. It was during his time serving on the commission to try the Lancashire rebels in 1715–16 that he began to acquire a reputation as a 'hanging judge', a reputation which was not helped by his overseeing the high-profile accusation of murder against the poet Richard Savage which brought him to the attention of the literati of the day; Pope, Hogarth and Doctor Johnson all criticised and satirised him. Not without reason: Savage was found guilty of murder following an impassioned, and highly partisan, speech to the jury from Page, although he was later pardoned after numerous pleas to the Crown from his well-placed friends. Savage gained his revenge by publishing a critique of the trial in which he wrote of Page:

> Of heart impure and impotent of head,
> In history, rhetoric, ethics, law unread;
> How far unlike such worthies, once a drudge –
> From floundering in law causes – rose a judge.

Because of the vitriol Page faced during his lifetime it is difficult to assess how much he actually deserved such a legacy, but one recorded incident from his life may offer a clue. A humorous barrister named Crowle was asked on entering Page's court one morning 'I suppose the Judge is just behind?' 'I hope so,' replied Crowle, 'he was never just before'.

Page died in 1742 and was buried in a mausoleum he had commissioned beside Steeple Aston Church; in building his monument he had a number of existing tombs demolished to make space for his own memorial, something which doubtless did little to endear him to his neighbours. Why this mini-biography? Well, there is clearly an exorcism story which has been lost to history because I found this tantalising snippet in *The History of Steeple Aston and Middle Aston* by the Rev. C. C. Brookes:

> At midnight the ghosts of the widows of the hundred men he had hanged pursue him up and down the pond where his ghost was banished in a beer barrel, in the form of owls.

The inclusion of owls as the bird of choice for this vengeful haunting is probably because of the association of these birds as omens of bad luck or even death, but the idea of banishing a spirit to a barrel is surprisingly common.

The original Bampton Manor started life as a simple farmhouse before becoming the formal Manor in 1610 – the present building however only dates from the very early 1800s. Around this time, according to a letter in *Folklore* quoting a Mrs Hannah Wells, it was held by a gentleman by the name of Whittaker. Gentleman in title perhaps but his behaviour might suggest something rather different for Mr Whittaker, respectable married man though he was, seems to have taken something of a shine to a young girl in the village, much to the distress of his unfortunate wife. Despite all her pleadings her callous husband refused to break off his affair with his paramour and so the poor Mrs Whittaker fell into depression and eventually died of a broken heart.

Naturally, this was not the end of her story and her distressed spirit returned to haunt the manor, the scene of all her unhappy memories; whether from grief or for reasons of simple revenge is unknown. Whatever her motives, her shade made regular and noisy appearances in the property. Whittaker soon tired of all her nocturnal nagging and summoned a team of exorcist priests to banish the phantom. His godly ghostbusters were happy to oblige and banished the late Mrs Whittaker to the bottom of Calves Close Pond which lay nearby in the grounds of the Manor. Alas, one dry summer some years later the pond completely evaporated and the spirit was thereby released to pursue her posthumous peregrinations.

Clearly the return of a revenant wife would have been something of a passion-killer for Whittaker and his new young partner and so the exorcists were once again summoned to lay the ghost, this time for good. Mindful that a pond was an unreliable resting place the spirit was this time forced into a barrel of strong beer which was promptly sealed and then locked away in the cellar of the house where, one can only assume, it remains to this very day. Certainly, after that time Mrs Whittaker's ghost ceased to trouble her husband.

Sometimes there are surprising concordances and correspondences between ghost stories from different places: a generous observer might explain that ghost stories are clearly universal, a cynic might opt for the simple transposition of one story to another location whether deliberately or in error. Bear this in mind as we visit the village of Stanton Harcourt.

Some 300 years ago the Hall family lived at Manor Farm in Stanton Harcourt. Mr and Mrs Hall seemed to be a perfectly ordinary couple although after a while Mr Hall seems to have developed a taste for the ale served at the nearby Harcourt Arms Inn and began to spend increasingly long evenings enjoying the pleasures offered by its snug interior. Doubtless

The Harcourt Arms, location of Mr Hall's *affaire d'amour*

feeling somewhat excluded from her husband's new social life Mrs Hall did her best to persuade her errant husband to spend time at home, but to no avail and his evenings out continued unabated. Determined to put a stop to his drinking Mrs Hall followed him to the pub one evening only to make the unwelcome discovery that fine ales were not the only attraction that the Harcourt Arms had to offer; in fact the welcoming arms of the landlady Mrs Surman were also a large part of the entertainment available to her wayward husband.

Determined to put an end to the affair she confronted him with her knowledge of his adulterous behaviour in an attempt to shame him back to her side, but Mr Hall was not to be swayed and refused to break off his relationship with the landlady. Crushed and broken-hearted the unfortunate Mrs Hall took her own life by drinking poison. It is said that her last act was to rinse out her drinking cup at the village pump so that no-one else would accidentally swallow the dregs of her fateful, fatal draught.

As in the Bampton story, Mrs Hall refused to take her death lying down and returned to haunt the farmyard and garden of her former home as well as the tavern owned by her rival. She was eventually banished to a pond in the village which, it is said, never runs dry so any further exorcism should, in theory anyway, be unnecessary.

An aside in *Folklore* mentions 'There was a spirit "laid" in a barrel of beer at Stanton Harcourt, and the barrel had always to be kept full to prevent the spirit from returning.' Is this a different tale or a corollary to the story of Mrs Hall that parallels the previous account? Pub regulars claim that Mrs Hall has occasionally been glimpsed in more recent times, but since The Harcourt Arms was temporarily closed at the time of writing and used as a private house I was unable to investigate further.* The pub has now reopened so perhaps additional details may yet be forthcoming.

These are wonderful tales, echoing as they do the story of the shade of Squire Crowdy of Highworth who was (voluntarily)

---

* It is considered very poor form to follow up stories of this kind.
Investigator knocks on door: Hi, I would like to ask if you have ever seen the terrifying apparition which is said to haunt your house?
Homeowner: Er …?

confined to a barrel of cider and also hidden away in the cellars. There is also a rumour of a spirit confined to a barrel of wine which lies hidden in a cellar in Charlbury to this very day but the identity of the person whose spirit was so confined has been lost. And it is not just barrels ...

Sir Laurence Tanfield was born in what is now the Bay Tree Hotel in Burford, posthumously proving that not everything that comes out of an inn is necessarily a good thing. He was MP for Woodstock in the 1580s and '90s and later made Baron of the Exchequer. He bought Burford Priory which, along with the manors of Burford and Great Tew, he partially enclosed in 1622 making him deeply unpopular with the common people of these villages. If Sir Lawrence was disliked he seems to have been a model of popularity compared to his second wife Elizabeth, who was said to have promised to 'play the Devil' to their tenants and to 'grind them to powder' beneath the wheels of her carriage. Sir Lawrence died in 1625 and was buried in Burford Church – in a tomb his wife did not bother to seek ecclesiastical permission to build. It was said that he had to be buried at night to avoid provoking riotous protests; certainly, his effigy was burned in Burford High St on the anniversary of his death for the next 200 years. Interestingly, the Tanfields' tomb features a carved skeleton to illustrate mortality: unusually, one femur of the skeleton is not carved but is an actual human bone. No-one knows why.

When Elizabeth Tanfield followed her husband to the grave in 1629 the townsfolk thought that they were finally rid of the poisonous pair but were doubtless horrified when the couple returned in regular reappearances, riding a fiery coach across the skies above the town cursing and insulting those below. Faced with such apparitional abuse the townsfolk sought spiritual assistance and Lady Tanfield's ghost (for clearly, she was the driving force behind the haunting) was banished to a wine bottle which was cast into the River Windrush only to come to rest underneath the third arch of the village bridge. A wine bottle is not such a secure prison as a beer barrel and, as late as Victorian times, when the water level dropped too low local people were seen throwing buckets of water over this archway, allegedly in an attempt to ensure that the cork did not dry out thus freeing the spectre once more.

THE OX-FILES

The Tanfield Tomb

Many years later Lord and Lady Tanfield were seen driving a carriage drawn by fire-breathing horses, not in the sky in this case but along the lane between Wilcote and North Leigh. The old man who reported this sighting described how his horse began to tremble and froth at the mouth in fear as the apparition passed – even though it was entirely blind. Presumably the water level in the Windrush was especially low that night.

The prevalence of these stories of ghosts laid to rest in barrels and the like is clearly a long-running and deep-rooted belief both in the local area and beyond. As long ago as 1848 William Ferguson, a Minister of the Congregational Church in Bicester, wrote a book titled *The Impending Dangers of Our Country: Or, Hidden Things Brought to Light* in which he lamented the state of the church which had allowed superstition and belief in the supernatural to prosper. He wrote derisively:

> We have been gravely informed by some of our neighbours that the best way to keep [a ghost] out of sight is to cause him to enter into a barrel of ale!

In a letter in similar vein writing in the *Methodist Magazine* some years earlier Samuel Thorrowgood had stated;

> It has been truly said that there are Farmers and many others in Oxfordshire whose faith in Charmers, Ghosts and Fortune-tellers is much stronger and more productive than their faith in Christ! The Ghost, to use the language of the peasantry, is generally laid in a barrel of beer.

Given that beliefs of this kind were clearly endemic in the past we can only wonder at how many similar stories from the county may have been lost over the years.

The black panther sculpture of Charlbury

Beastly Behaviour

A DRAMATIC HEADLINE APPEARED in the *Oxford Mail* on 19 March 2005 which read, '*£5,000 to trap the Beast of Burford*'. The beast in question was a large black cat which had been seen on many occasions around the town up to that point and the reward had been offered by the Cotswold Wildlife Park who were keen to acquire the animal for their collection and, as a not-entirely-unrelated benefit, prove that the creature wasn't one of their escapees. But perhaps we need to rewind just a touch for some background.

Mysterious large black cats[*] have been sighted across Oxfordshire for many years but with especial frequency in the west of the county. After a stuttering start in 1997 when a large cat in a tree scared two anglers near Abingdon and another was sighted crossing a road near Culham and subsequently sporadically reported around the village, the story moved firmly north-west.

In June 1999 an animal described as 'about the size of a medium-sized fox or deer, but it was definitely a cat' dashed across the road in front of a car near Crawley, just north of Witney. Note that the animal's colour is not mentioned but the references to foxes and deer might suggest brown – although

---

[*] OK, a slight diversion here. Why describe them in that order? There is an unspoken but powerful rule in English that adjectives are always used in the order: opinion, size, age, shape, colour, origin, material, purpose. So a black, mysterious large cat breaks the rule and sounds decidedly odd to the ear. This is called the royal order of adjectives and it is just as mysterious as anything else within these pages. Try it with any piece of purple prose from this book. The small, aged, white apparition moved slowly towards her ...

after a nearly identical sighting in the same area lorry driver Malcolm Dix did describe the animal as being black. Six months later, in January 2000, Anne Lovell was driving near Minster Lovell* when she also encountered the animal. 'I know it wasn't a fox as I had just seen one earlier,' she commented. 'I caught it in the headlights and it looked tawny in colour. It was much bigger than a fox or a domestic cat.' If this was the same animal it had clearly grown; if not it looked as if there might be a minor moggie menagerie on the prowl. It (or they) was also extending its range; there were reports of a large black cat the following month from both Kennington and Shotover Park.

So, after a meandering introduction, we move to the meat of the story. Although sightings continued to be reported occasionally, it wasn't until a few years later that the story came back to life with a spate of sightings of what soon became dubbed as *The Beast of Burford* from villages around the area and the discovery of a deer with the flesh stripped from its legs and claw marks on its body – along with the suspicion (hotly denied) that the animal might have been an escapee from the Cotswold Wildlife Park. Local farmer Nick August described his encounter in February 2005. 'At first I presumed it was a dog, but when I saw it side on it looked like a very big cat, completely black and with a large tail'. Probably a frightening enough description to make local people nervous, especially when more killings were reported by farmer Colin Daws: 'It's taking big sheep so it must be a powerful animal,' he commented, ominously. In any case, as we have already observed, at this point the Park offered a reward for the capture of the animal, director Reggie Heyworth announcing in March: 'If anybody can capture this large cat and it's the real McCoy, not a large feral dog or a large domestic cat, and they can do it by Easter, we'll give them £5,000. We've got a cage waiting for it.' Even the Channel 4 *Richard and Judy* show joined in, adding a thousand pounds to the prize pot for anyone who could produce a convincing photograph.

Big cat expert Danny Nineham, who had many years' experience of tracking ABCs** all across the UK, visited the

---

* No relation.
** Alien Big Cats.

area but doubted that the animal could be caught without using live bait, something that is illegal in the UK. He suggested that the animal could be a panther and added some words of wisdom concerning the variety of sightings that had been reported. 'Panther is just a nickname for a black leopard. The reason people spot them is because they're so black, they stick out like a sore thumb in the countryside, while a puma is tawny so it's harder to see.' So there may well be the chance of more than one type of cat after all.

And so the stage was set for the arrival of an even more impressive figure in April: big game hunter John Collinson. Well, that is how he was described in the headlines. In reality Collinson, who lived in Charlbury, had been a warden at the Ugalla Game Reserve in western Tanzania from 1948 to the 1970s, where he followed the trails of big cats like lions and leopards as a conservationist not a hunter. His verdict? 'It's possibly a cat, but it's not certain. What I'm looking for is whether there are any claw marks. If there are, it's most likely to be a dog, as cats have retractable claws [...] Leopards don't like exposing themselves to people, they're more private than a lion or a cheetah, but they will always adapt themselves to where they're living.'

Sadly, Collinson's expertise proved no more useful than Nineham's and the Beast remained at large; certainly, reports of it still being alive continued to arrive. George Gasiorowski spotted it near Church Hanborough, describing how the animal sniffed around before it saw him and ran into the wood. 'Across the field, near the opening of the wood, there was this black, beautiful animal, about 250 to 300 yards away [...] It was too big for a domestic cat – about two or three times bigger – and had a long tail, unlike anything I've ever seen on a normal cat.' Bucking the trend another witness described a sandy-coloured animal in fields near Bampton in May 2006 demonstrating, if nothing else, the existence of the missing lynx ...

For a while the story died down again, but more reports started coming forward in 2011 after the unveiling of a plaster cast of another big cat paw print taken from an undisclosed west Oxfordshire location by a local policeman. He also admitted having stumbled upon 300m of big cat tracks back in 2007. While local interest simmered gently the story briefly boiled over into the national news in 2014 when Isabel Oakeshott, the political editor of *The Sunday Times*, tweeted: 'I just saw something very like a black panther in woods near Charlbury.' This high-profile sighting was almost immediately countered by the local Priory House Trust, who revealed that they had a sculpture of a puma made by artist Simon Lea in their gardens which had probably been the source of the report. Mr Lea explained that the inspiration for the puma piece had actually been his own encounter with the beast. 'I was walking through woods and suddenly I was aware of something. It was enormous – so quick. It crossed the path and walked through the trees in seconds.' Police admitted that the sculpture, which was clearly visible from passing trains, generated regular 'beast' reports.*

And although the main Beast of Burford craze had largely run its course by that point occasional reports continued to come in. It popped up, somewhat out of its normal range, in 2016 when a teenager spotted it outside a pub in Marston;** Lisa London watched it crossing a road near Bicester in 2017 commenting, 'it essentially strolled across the road from the right to the left then leapt into the bushes. It looked like a black panther – it was shiny black and there was no way it was a dog or a deer or a domestic cat, it was too big'; a lorry driver managed to photograph it (from a considerable distance) shortly afterwards.

That same year a woman in Arncott spotted a large black cat crossing a road in front of her car. This was one of a series of sightings from the area and for a while the *'Beast of Otmoor'* was also a subject of lively debate. Given the distance between the Otmoor and Burford sightings I think we can be confident that these are *different* Beasts …

And then, in 2018, the Burford cat seemed to have found a mate. The Graingers, a couple who rather enviably spend their summers living on a narrow boat, were passing Culham Lock when they had their encounter. 'There was one sitting on its hind legs in the field when another came out of the woods and started nuzzling it. They were both jet black and bigger than

---

* It has since been moved to a less visible location.
** I doubt it came for a pint of Pawland's Original. (Other animal-related beer puns are available.)

a Labrador' commented Mr Grainger. 'I have good eyesight and they were no more than 100 metres away. I know what I saw – it was unmistakable.' The new pair sparked other reports both from near Radley and back to the more traditional area of Hook Norton.

Given that the lifespan of a big cat of this size is 10–20 years it does seem possible, despite the – er – paucity of physical evidence, that there is a continually reproducing population in Oxfordshire. The most popular theory is that the original cats were released into the wild by unscrupulous owners in 1976 following the introduction of the Dangerous Wild Animals Act which made keeping such creatures much more onerous. Other suggestions are that undocumented animals regularly escape from wherever they are being secretly (and clearly insecurely) held or, if we want to stick strictly to the *paranormal* theme, that the animals are either being mysteriously transported to the British countryside from parts unknown or are somehow supernatural in nature. Believe whichever you will.

And then in March 2020 came sad news, with a report from Olli Astley who was driving along the A34 near Kidlington and saw what he described as a 'black or dark brown puma or lynx-sized cat' lying dead on the central reservation. It had disappeared when reporters tried to locate it the following day so perhaps it had vanished back to the dimension from which it had originated – or maybe the council had picked up the corpse. Either way a sad story, but not the worst thing to happen in 2020.

Was this the end of the story of the Beast of Burford? Naturally not. The following month Hannah Millin filmed the cat on a mobile phone near Brize Norton. 'I know what a black cat looks like and I swear to God it was not a cat. It had a squarish face and was walking like a lion. I've never seen anything like this before.' And in January 2021 a cyclist encountered an unidentified black cat early one morning near Witney. The story goes on ...

The Bird in Hand, local inn of ill-repute in the eighteenth century;
haunt of the infamous Dunsdon brothers

Not Just Any Tom, Dick and Harry

AND ON TO HIGHWAYMEN, although not exactly the dashing Dick Turpin variety. Some writers claim that the unlikely trio of Tom, Dick and Harry Dunsdon* were born in a house in Minster Lovell but this is only partly true; they were born in a cottage in nearby Fulbrook which was later demolished and the stones used to build a larger property in Minster Lovell. Fulbrook was clearly not one of the better addresses in the county, as is shown by this local contemporary rhyme:

> *Fulbrook Suggs,*
> *Born in tubs,*
> *Couldn't get out,*
> *For lice and bugs.*

The oldest brother, Richard, was born in 1745 and seems to have been the ringleader of the group; it was probably under his influence that they forsook whatever passed for civilised society in their home village and retreated to a cottage at Icombe which, according to local legend at least, had a secret underground passage to a cave where they would keep the horses on which they made their living as highwaymen. Some story-tellers hold that they would shoe their horses with the horseshoes pointing backward to confuse those trying to track their movements.

The brothers started out as small-time criminals with a string of petty thefts to their name but gradually grew bolder

---

* It has been suggested that this trio are the origin of the eponymous phrase but this actually pre-dates them by some centuries – in fact the English theologian John Owen used the expression as long ago as 1657. An equally common alternate contemporary usage was Tom, Dick and Jack.

and greedier, eventually graduating to holding up the Oxford to Gloucester coach and gaining £500 for their trouble. This made them notorious locally, but also made them a much higher priority for the forces of law and order.

The inn known as The Bird in Hand, hard up against the edge of the Wychwood Forest, had an unsavoury reputation in the eighteenth century as a cock-fighting den and the haunt of local ne'er-do-wells (it was still known locally as 'the gambling house' as late as 1903) but of course this only made it all the more attractive to the three brothers. While at The Bird in Hand one evening they were overheard planning a scheme to rob nearby Tangley Hall while the Squire was away and one of the other drinkers warned the butler of the house about the proposed burglary. He called in the constables who were therefore lying in wait for the Dunsdons as they crept stealthily towards the property the following night. The front door of the Hall was constructed of stout oak with a small hatch which could be opened to inspect prospective visitors who came a-knocking at the door. Richard quietly slid the shutter aside and groped his arm inside feeling for a latch, at which point the butler slipped a rope around his wrist, looped it around the handle inside and shouted for the constables. To avoid his capture, Tom and Harry were forced to hack their brother's arm off at the shoulder and flee into the night.

Not surprisingly, Richard did not survive the ad-hoc amputation and died shortly afterwards. His brothers continued their criminal careers,[*] graduating swiftly from robbery to murder: early one morning a ditch digger stumbled upon the brothers while they were burying a body at a remote clearing in the forest and they killed him on the spot and buried him in the same grave.

Eventually The Bird in Hand was to be their downfall. One evening they were deep in their cups and loudly bragging that they were such hard men that 'no-one could take them'. Hearing this boast the landlord, a man named Benjamin Paget who fancied that he was on good enough terms with the brothers

---

[*] I am not sure why the younger Dunsden brothers never came under suspicion for the Tangley Hall robbery as it was clear that Richard had had a hand in it ...

to attempt a joke, responded that it would be no problem for *him* to bring them to justice should he be of a mind to do so. Unfortunately the brothers were either scared enough, paranoid enough or just plain drunk enough, to take him seriously and they shot the poor man on the spot. Luckily for Paget he had a pocket full of coins which, in an amazing stroke of luck or providence, deflected the bullet away from his heart. The other drinkers at the inn fell upon the Dunstons and held them until they could be arrested. (In an alternative version of the story the shot man is called William Harding and after the shooting the brothers were held by the landlord and other pub regulars.) Whichever version you prefer to believe, they were taken away to Gloucester for trial (the area looked to Gloucestershire for justice at the time) and hanged in 1784. Tom's leg had been injured during their capture and he struggled to make it to the scaffold; apparently Harry expressed little sympathy for his condition, telling him to stop complaining as he wouldn't have to stand on it for much longer.

Moving deeper into Wychwood there was a tavern known as the Hit and Miss public house (its pub sign, showing a man shooting at a pheasant and just catching its tail feathers in the blast, hinted at the poaching proclivities of its clientele) on the Fulbrook to Shipton road near a place known as Millin's Oak, and it was here that the brothers were gibbetted after being cut down. The initials HD and TD were carved into the trunk of the tree to commemorate the event. The ghost of Richard Dunsdon has been seen flitting between the inn and the tree on occasion. At least it is assumed to be Richard's ghost; why else would the phantom be described as having only one arm?

Millin's Oak, also commonly known as the Gibbet Tree, still stands near Hensgrove Wood and has an interesting story of its own. John Millin was the local gamekeeper who was out watching for trespassers one night when he was shot by a poacher (who had mistaken him for a deer in the dark) and left for dead. He was found by two other men named Pittaway and James (who were also poaching in the woods) but they at least had the decency to take him to Swinbrook and leave him at the Hit and Miss until a doctor could be summoned. Sadly, their act of charity was to cost them their lives; Millin died and the two men were arrested, charged with murder and hanged. On the scaffold Pittaway turned to the crowd and said 'Ah gentlemen, we be as innocent as the child just born.'

Many years later a Filkins man named Richard Cross made a death-bed confession that he and his partner, William Gillett, had been the cause of John Millin's death. In Cross's account Gillett had fired the fatal shot but the pair had sworn a solemn oath to take the secret to their graves. Gillett had, in fact died not long after the murder but Cross's revelations came, of course, far too late to save the unfortunate Pittaway and James.

Millin's Oak again had, for many years, the initials JM carved

Millin's Oak

into its bark to commemorate the death of the gamekeeper: the nearby inn is now a private house. A local man maintained the carved initials well into the 1930s but, in a reflection on both the resilience and transience of both fame and infamy, the carved initials can no longer be discerned.

Wychwood inns were clearly dangerous places. During a period of economic depression in the early 1840s known as the 'hungry forties' Mr Goodman, the landlord of the Crown Inn at Finstock, was so nervous of being robbed that he had the top part of the door at the top of his stairs removed so that he could see above it and shoot any intruders who might be inclined to come upstairs with burglary in mind. Clearly his fears were not exaggerated as, on hearing a noise from the bar area one night, he grabbed a large fork as a weapon and burst into the room just in time to see a man with a blackened face climbing in through the window. The man fled but was identified the following day by the village shopkeeper who noticed traces of lampblack still on his face. Despite this, perhaps because of the close-knit nature of the local community, it seems that the man was never prosecuted for the attempted break-in.

In a sadder story, a traveller staying at the Crown had stopped at the nearby Bull Inn for a drink where a number of local ruffians, who had spotted the fullness of his wallet, resolved to have its contents for themselves. As he walked back to the Crown he was set upon and murdered. Because he had hidden his wallet in the lining of his coat this was not found by his killers although they did take his hat, a mistake which cost them their own lives when it was later recognised. The man's horse dutifully returned to the Crown where it too was recognised, and a search party dispatched to discover what had happened to him. His body was recovered and suitably buried, but his ghost haunted the Crown for some years afterwards.

A similar tale is told of the Shipton Inn at Shipton-under-Wychwood, this one dating from around 1850. In this case a stranger arrived at the inn and took lodgings with the intention of visiting the annual fair at Leafield the following day. Asking after a guide some village lads offered to escort him there after dark; the fact that they had marked him as well-to-do, and the owner of a rather valuable gold watch to boot, having strongly influenced their offer.

Next day the unknown visitor was discovered wounded and bleeding in the forest by a man cutting brushwood. He was taken to the inn but died shortly afterwards. He is buried in a grave in the churchyard marked simply as 'unknown man'.

The traveller from a little earlier may not have been lucky enough to reach the village of Leafield but had he done so he may have decided to stay at The Fox inn which can also, of course, boast that it hosts the story of a ghost.

In this case the ghost is said to be that of a married woman who, in the later years of the eighteenth century, took a lover with whom she would frolic at The Fox. Unfortunately for the adulterous couple the deceived husband found out about the relationship and resolved to bring an end to the affair. Consequently, one day he told his wife that he was going away on a trip while in fact hiding and then secretly following her to The Fox where she had arranged to meet her lover. Once he knew where the couple met, he was able to burst into the room and murder his rival just before their next assignation. When she arrived for her next visit, the wife discovered the lifeless body of her paramour but, having little other choice, was forced to return to the marital home and resume life with her husband. Not unnaturally, it seems as if she was unable to cope with the grief associated with her loss, nor presumably with the knowledge that the man with whom she shared a home had murdered her lover in cold blood. Unable to bear her situation, she crept from the house one night and hanged herself in the forest.

Of course, no good story could ever end here, and her restless spirit is said to return to The Fox, presumably hoping to be reunited with the spirit of her murdered lover. Her appearances come in a number of forms; sometimes she appears as a shadowy figure beside the fireplace in the bar whilst at other times she seems a solid-looking figure dressed in a cloak and high riding boots. Whatever her aspect she shows a blithe disregard for furniture or even walls, striding casually through all obstacles in her way, leaving the faint but unmistakable scent of lavender in her wake and a decided chill in the air.

Some witnesses report that this enigmatic figure wears a haughty or annoyed expression on her occasional appearances; perhaps she is becoming frustrated at her late lover's continual non-appearance.

Oxfordshire Rocks

OXFORDSHIRE IS WELL ENDOWED with standing stones of all varieties, circles, clusters and lone sentinels all grace the landscape, but by far the best known are the Rollright Stones. The site is first documented in the fourteenth-century *De Mirabilibus Britanniae* [*The Wonders of Britain*]: 'In the neighbourhood of Oxford there are great stones, arranged as it were in some connection by the hand of man. But at what time; or by what people; or for what memorial or significance, is unknown'. This collection of 'great stones' consisting of a single standing King Stone, tumbledown collection of Whispering Knights and King's Men stone circle are so far to the north that the county can barely claim them as its own; the legend behind them stretches into nearby Warwickshire.

According to local folklore the stones are the petrified remains of a king and his army who were, for reasons unknown but we can probably assume invasion and conquest, marching across north Oxfordshire when they were confronted by a witch. Clearly recognising their nefarious ambitions, the witch issued something of a cross between a prophecy and a challenge to the king.

> Seven long strides shalt thou take, and if Long Compton thou canst see, King of England thou shalt be.

Knowing that the village would easily be visible from the top of the hill the King strode forward shouting: 'Stick, stock, stone,* as King of England I shall be known!' Seven stately strides later and preparing to gaze down on the village, the King was horrified to discover that his sight was blocked by a barrow

---

* Worst recipe for soup, ever.

which obscured his view of the valley below. The witch then cackled (I may have added that detail myself) and said:

> As Long Compton thou canst not see King of England thou shalt not be.
> Rise up, stick, and stand still, stone, for King of England thou shalt be none,
> Thou and thy men hoar stones shall be and I myself an elder tree.

At which point the king was transformed into the King Stone, his army (who were presumably maypole dancing at the time) became the Rollright Stone circle and a group of knights who had gathered off to one side, supposedly plotting treachery, became the Whispering Knights.

Everyone knows this legend, but what is rather less well-known is the fact that it has evolved considerably over the years. The story is first documented in Camden's 1586 *Britannia*, 'the common people usually call them Rolle-rick stones,* and dreameth that they were sometimes men by a wonderful Metamorphosis turned into hard stones.' According to the version of the story documented in the 1705 *Natural History of Oxfordshire*, by Dr. R. Plot, the two protagonists are a Danish king and a Saxon general (who also doubles as a wizard). By the time Arthur Evans published the version above in *Folklore* in 1895, the witch was firmly established as the saviour of the realm. There is even a corollary to the story that, at some unspecified point in time, the petrification will wear off and the King and his army will once more be free to maraud across the land. If that does happen I'm not sure who will be most surprised ...

Interestingly, although the various stones are all associated with the same legend today, they actually date from different periods of prehistory. The Whispering Knights are the remains of an early Neolithic burial mound (much like Weyland's Smithy at the opposite end of the county) whereas the stone circle is around a thousand years younger, having been constructed around 2500BC. The lone King Stone is of uncertain date and may be related to the circle or may have been erected separately.

---

* Never gonna give you up ...

The Rollright Stone circle: the King's Men

Naturally, there is considerable other miscellaneous folklore associated with the site. The most common belief is that the stones in the King's Men circle are uncountable and that anyone trying to do so will never be able to reach the same total twice but, should they ever manage to do so, their dearest wish will be granted; certainly a trip or two around the circle demonstrates how this belief might have originated. Naturally this belief presented a challenge and once upon a time a baker decided to settle any numerical arguments once and for all. Bringing samples of his wares to the site he circled around the stones leaving a piece of bread on each marker as he counted it off so that, once he had made a full circle, he had managed to count the definitive number. Unfortunately for us, and even more so for him, before he was able to reveal the correct total the Devil appeared and whisked him off to hell for his presumption.* Perhaps the Satanic security has now been removed, or perhaps the periodic stealing of stones for local buildings has made the matter moot, but British archaeologist Aubrey Burl wrote of 'seventy-seven stones, stumps and lumps of leprous limestone' without suffering any infernal infelicity.

---
* So much for *his* dearest wish.

Stealing the stones may well have presented a problem since they are notoriously difficult to remove. Many years ago a local farmer decided to use one of the larger, flatter megaliths to construct a bridge across a stream on his land and so dug around the base and hitched two horses to the stone to attempt to drag it away. They were not up to the task and he was forced to add more and more horses to the yoke – eventually the stone grudgingly began to move when he had a full score of horses pulling in unison. Even then the story did not end well; as he attempted to set it in place the stone toppled over, crushing him to death. To make matters worse when local people returned to use the bridge the following day it had flipped itself over to the bank of the stream nearest the circle. Twice they returned it to its position across the stream and twice more each morning it was found beside the bank. Acknowledging that they were beaten they prepared to undertake the arduous task of dragging the stone back to its original position and were amazed when it took only one horse to move the rock – even uphill. In folkloric terms this makes this a 'stubborn stone'.

Perhaps because of its position of splendid isolation,* many of the local stories focus on the King Stone. Writing in *Folklore* Arthur Evans (who would later achieve fame through his excavations of Knossos in Crete) interviewed an old man who told him that his friend Will Hughes had once seen fairies whom he described as 'little folk like girls to look at' dancing around the King Stone. Hughes' 80-year-old widow Betsy revealed that when she was a little girl she had known of a gap in the bank close to the King Stone, from whence fairies emerged to dance at night. In the spirit of enquiry (or perhaps simple fear) Betsy and her friends had tried covering the hole with a stone at night to keep the fairies trapped inside but they always found the blockage removed the following morning. Evans also wrote of how a generation before that, the local people would gather on Midsummer Eve, when the elder tree was in blossom, form a circle around the King Stone and cut the elder. As the tree 'bled' the King Stone would 'turn its head'.

---

* Well, it's across the road anyway.

Evans also relates two conflicting beliefs about the efficacy of collecting stone chips, from the King Stone in particular. One thread contends that a piece will bring good luck, the other advises that ill fortune will follow any surreptitious snick-snatchers. Betsy Hughes told him that her son had taken a shard with him to India for luck – although the luck turned out to be anything but good since he ended up dying of typhus. A different, older, story tells of how another vandal found the wheels of his wagon immovably frozen until he replaced the stolen shard. Certainly, the Rollright Trust which owns the site would prefer to promote the bad-luck version of the legend.

Evans commented that 'it would be difficult to find any English site where folklore is more living at the present day' and this probably still applies today. Writing in the 1920s Alfred Watkins, father of the Ley Line, described an alignment running through Long Compton church, the Rollright Stones, Chipping Norton church and a tumulus near Charlbury. Another runs due south through the Squires Clump round barrow at Sarsden, Lyneham long barrow, Ascott long barrow, Brize Norton church and on to Faringdon Folly Summit and then the Uffington White Horse. Clearly this is a nexus of significant earth energies.* Certainly the stones, especially the King Stone, have been the focus of any number of Wiccan ceremonies since the 1960s at least. One recent visitor described finding flowers and petals scattered around the main circle: a pagan offering or fairy detritus?

Moving speculation in a more scientific direction, Paul Devereux's Dragon Project used Geiger counters and electromagnetic detectors to investigate the stones, discovering that the King Stone seemed to emit a pulse of ultrasound at sunrise and that there were odd geomagnetic patterns to be found within the circle itself. In a parallel series of experiments researchers slept at the site to see, quite literally, what dreams might come. This is almost a throwback to earlier times when young girls from the surrounding villages would climb up onto the Knights 'to hear what they might be whispering'.

There is one other legend we ought to mention concerning both the King and the Knights: at midnight or Midsummer's

---

* Well, maybe.

Eve (or some other significant Saint's Day depending on the version of the tale), the stones lift themselves out of the ground and troop down to Little Rollright to drink at a nearby spring. Local children who misbehaved were warned that the stones would collect them on the way back from their drinking and take them away to become part of the circle. An alternative version of the tale has them dancing.* (Incidentally, do not attempt to observe any of this ambulatory activity as it will either send you mad or kill you outright.) Of course, why the stones should exhibit this behaviour is not clear, but it is a trait shared by a number of other local megaliths.

If the Rollrights are the Stonehenge of Oxfordshire, then our local Avebury must surely be the much lesser-known Devil's Quoits. The analogy is actually remarkably accurate as The Quoits, which can be found near Stanton Harcourt,** were one of the largest circles in the country comprising 36 stones surrounded by a henge earthwork with a circle diameter of almost 80 metres. Unfortunately, theft from the site for building material began in Roman times, with further damage from ploughing and stone pilfering occurring throughout the mediaeval period. By the time F. P. Palmer and A. H. Forrester were writing *The Wanderings of a Pen and Pencil* in 1846 there were only three stones still standing. 'Them be the devil's kites!' said the guide; 'a many year ago they carried a bigger than all on 'em away, to make a bridge somewhere.' Very much an echo of the Rollrights story. A decade later Dicken's *Dictionary of the Thames* mentions only two stones and by the time the site was used for a Second World War airfield there was but a single stone. Even this was toppled when the whole area was used for gravel extraction during the 1970s.

The origin of the Quoits is clear in the name. One Sunday the Devil was entertaining himself with a game of quoits near Eynsham when God appeared and told him to stop enjoying himself on the Sabbath. In a fit of pique the devil hurled his play pieces away and they formed the circle where they landed. An alternative version has the Devil playing with an itinerant

---
* The stones, not the children.
** Stan-tun meaning village of the stones – Harcourt refers to the local landowners.

pedlar and the Quoits remained behind after their game. There is a quite different legend which explains that the stones are all that remains of wedding guests who were turned to stone for dancing on a Sunday. That would explain the circular shape at least. The Quoits even have a story to directly parallel that of the Rollrights in that a farmer once took a stone for a bridge across a stream called the 'Black Ditch' but was forced to replace it after it refused to remain in place and kept slipping into the stream. Not only that, but like the Rollrights, the stones are sometimes said to migrate en masse down to the River Chew to drink at midnight. Local parents here would also scare their children by telling them that if they were naughty these stones too would come and abduct them from their beds and take them away to join the circle.*

In any case, the present circle has had to be completely rebuilt just adjacent to its original site although the reconstruction, done in the early 2000s, may contain a few rescued original stones.

There is even a third circle at Stonor Park. This monument is generally thought to have been a fairly recent construction (either seventeenth or twentieth century depending on which source you believe) although the stones themselves may well have come from an earlier, genuine, circle situated on the land the chapel now occupies. 'Christianisation' of old sites was once a common phenomenon so this may well be a valid theory.

Oxfordshire may have two (or three) circles but it can also boast of a plethora of individual standing stones. The Hoar Stone in Enstone, actually a collection of stones which will originally have formed the entrance to a barrow (and which are said to be the remains of a man, his horse and his dog who were punished for hunting on a Sunday) is also reputed to head off to drink, as is the Hawk Stone at Chadlington. Incidentally, the names of both derive from the Old English 'har' meaning old or grey; indeed, the Hawk Stone is sometimes called the Old Soldier and the largest stone of the Enstone group is referred to as the Old General. The Hoar Stone and companions come complete with a legend that they are the last remaining vestiges of a city which once stood on the site and that should any of

---

* Whether the stones came a-calling or not I'm sure the result would still be petrified children.

Chadlington Hawk Stone

them be moved then they will always return to their proper place. Sadly, I know of no evidence which might support either of these assertions. In contrast the Hawk Stone was supposed to have been either dragged or thrown into place by a local witch. Given this origin it seems unfair to claim the notch in the top of the stone was the result of chafing from the chains used for binding witches to it before they were burned.

Confusingly, there used to be yet another Hoar Stone near Steeple Barton which had the reputation of always returning if moved. Unfortunately, due to its folkloric reputation the farmer who owned the land broke it up in the mid-nineteenth century, but local people for many years held the belief that the individual parts were regrowing. An older name for the stone was the Maiden's Bower, possibly indicating that previous generations would have found more complete remains of a chambered tomb.

There is an un-named marker stone between Enstone and Clevely with few traditional tales attached but which, according to writer Celia Haddon, does have a modern twist to an old legend. While walking in the area she met a man walking his dog and they fell to discussing the stone. 'The farmer had removed it but they made him put it back,' commented the man. Supernatural agency has clearly now been replaced by local government. Or possibly, operating through local bureaucracy is now the preferred working method *of* supernatural agency ...

One odd stone we haven't mentioned is the Blowing Stone at Kingston Lisle described by Thomas Hughes in *Tom Brown's Schooldays* as 'square lump of stone some three feet and a half high, perforated with two or three queer holes, like petrified antediluvian rat-holes'. Reputed to have been used by King Alfred to summon his troops to battle, this stone can indeed produce (if you blow into the correct hole and have the right technique) what Hughes describe as a 'grewsome [sic] sound between a moan and a roar [...] a ghost-like awful voice'. Clearly the ability to summon armies meant that it had no need to move; besides, it sits alongside what was for many years the Blowing Stone Inn.

Two local stones are possessed of secret tunnels. One, at Langley Farm in the Wychwood Forest, is reputed to have a tunnel leading to Minster Lovell Hall; another, at Lyneham Barrow near Chipping Norton, is possessed of a subterranean passage down to the local river, thus cleverly avoiding the need to be seen going down for a drink perhaps.

And, apropos of nothing, let us just take a moment to appreciate the sarsens known as the Druid Stones scattered around Ashdown House on the Ridgeway. No rumours of movement, no curses and no secret tunnels but perhaps this is not surprising: the stones are said to be the remains of sheep petrified by the wizard Merlin himself. What they had done to deserve this punishment is unknown; perhaps they were grazing somewhere they shouldn't. In similar wise, there was once an old woman who was in the habit of allowing her flock of geese to wander as they would in the fields around Chastleton and, despite being warned of the consequences, she refused to stop them doing so. As a result her geese were subsequently transformed into what are now called the Goose Stones. Although many have now been removed, they have not been observed returning.

Sheldonian heads waiting for their moment to make a move

And finally, the Thor Stone near Taston may share an etymology with the Hoar Stone (although perhaps not, given that the local village was recorded as Thorstan in 1278), but because of its name the legend has arisen that it is the result of a thunderstone hurled by the thunder god Thor. It may not move now but it must have put the shuffling-to-drink crowd to shame when it did.

It isn't only prehistoric monuments which seem to display a disturbing tendency to roam. There is a legend that the carved heads outside the Sheldonian Theatre in Oxford leave their places and dance with the University Proctors at midnight and, although I haven't been able to find a Proctor who will admit to having undertaken anything so risqué, I did a quick check though and there is nothing to actually forbid dancing with university statues in the university statutes.

One piece of stonework with a rather more sedate movement is the effigy of Lady Elizabeth Blackett who died in 1442 and who lies with her husband Sir William Wylcot (one-time Sheriff of Berkshire and Oxfordshire) in the Wilcote Chapel of North Leigh Church. The hands of the pair are raised in prayer but it is said that Lady Elizabeth's are gradually moving apart.

Lady Elizabeth Blackett and her husband Sir William Wylcot

Once they have moved entirely out of their position of prayer local people claimed that either her ghost would return or some other terrible (unspecified) event would occur. Thankfully, they seem to be moving very slowly indeed.

And as one final example of shifting stonework, the spherical decorations atop the gateposts to Charney Bassett Manor are reputed to leave their position at midnight and rumble around the perimeter walls. Now that's rock and roll.

The Bull at Burford

A Relatively Haunted Hotel

Great Tew, Little Tew, Enstone and Barford,
If you want a pretty girl, you must go to Burford.

CLEARLY LONG RENOWNED for the attractiveness of its local ladies Burford was also famous for the behaviour of its menfolk – there is an old expression *'to take a Burford bait'*, the bait in question being a bout (of sickness): in other words to be *very* hungover. Luckily, and perhaps not coincidentally, should you require aspirin or Alka Seltzer Burford is the home of Britain's oldest pharmacy.

Burford Antiques was one of the establishments frequented by the notorious Dunsdon brothers (although it was known as the George Inn at the time, the Dunsdons having little interest in the *legitimate* acquisition of antiques) and, in a weird coincidence, as the bodies of Tom and Dick were being returned from Gloucester to be gibbetted in the Wychwood Forest the cart driver given this unenviable task stopped here for a drink on his way to Millin's Oak. Clearly the spirits of the two brothers considered this an ideal stopping off point and have haunted the building ever since, causing assorted banging and scraping sounds to be heard from the upper floors late at night. One of the stallholders reported an incident some years ago while she was locking up for the day, when her dog suddenly crouched down and started to growl. Although the building was completely empty she was horrified to watch the dog's gaze follow someone or something climbing invisibly up the stairs.

But I digress. The Hannes family who ran the Bull at Burford Hotel (originally The Bull Inn and sited slightly further along the High St than its present location) in the mid-1500s were listed as vintners and so this was clearly one of the better inns in the town. When the family moved out of innkeeping the business passed to a tenant, John Silvister, who took the name at least and re-established the Bull on its present spot in 1610, in a building that can be traced at least as far back as 1473. A pub of such long-standing provenance is bound to have picked up a ghost or two along the way and in the case of the Bull one of its hauntings seems to stem from the murder of an unnamed man by William Baxter during a brawl in the bar. Details are sketchy but the sounds of a scuffle have been heard, along with a fair degree of bad language, and the figures of two men, presumably the combatants, have also been spotted.

Whilst The Bull can boast a history of famously indiscreet couples (Lord Nelson and Lady Emma Hamilton stayed there as did Charles II and Nell Gwynne) it was also the scene of a much more local relationship scandal in 1765 when a farmer from just outside the town proposed to one of the serving girls in order to win a bet. Sadly, he was unwilling (and unable) to follow through on his promise and when the fact that he had failed to honour his engagement to the young girl became public knowledge he was subject to the traditional display of rural displeasure; a strong dose of 'rough music', which involved a very public shaming by neighbours banging pots and pans outside the culprit's home.

But back to ghosts. While a teenage girl some 50 years ago, Juliet Waldron was on holiday in the UK with her mother and staying at the Bull. According to her account she was allocated a room on the third floor.* At around 10pm she left her mother carousing downstairs in the bar, retreated to bed and fell quickly asleep. Briefly, anyway. She described what happened next:

> Next thing I knew, I was standing in the hall, a few steps beyond my door. The light had apparently gone out because it was pitch black. I was in my flannel nightgown. It was confusing, because I didn't know how I'd got there, and besides, it was uncomfortably

---

* Since she was visiting from the US I'm assuming that this equates to the second floor in real money.

cold. That was when I saw him, a gentleman with a moustache and beard, wearing a hat with a flowing plume and dressed in Restoration over-the-top garb. Weirdly, he was visible only to the shin. He bowed, removed his hat, and greeted me, saying that he was an ancestor who had been waiting there in Burford to see me for quite a long time.

Juliet commented that she wasn't frightened by the meeting, even though the figure seemed to have a strange glow coming from beneath his period clothing, but she did feel overwhelmed by the strangeness of the situation. Despite the statement from her self-proclaimed ancestor, she expressed the opinion that she was glimpsing him through a 'crack in time'. Suddenly, 'like a skipping track on a CD' the scene vanished and she found herself staring at the patterned wallpaper in the dimly-lit, but unmistakably modern, hotel corridor.

> Yes, I was in my nightgown, yes, it was icy cold, but my visitor was gone. I dashed back to my room, slammed the door and locked it, then jumped into bed and pulled the covers over my head. I thought I'd never go to sleep again, but I did.

The following morning she ventured out of her room and went downstairs for breakfast, relieved that the hotel seemed restored to normality in the bright summer morning sunlight. Over breakfast she excitedly told her mother about the events of the night and as she finished telling her story the proprietor came over and pulled a chair up to the table. 'Please whisper!' he said. 'He hasn't been seen up there for months, but he's not good for business so I don't want it to get around that he's back.' He then confessed that he had seen the apparition himself on numerous occasions and stressed that he believed that it would be bad for trade were rumours to spread that the inn was haunted. He seemed particularly interested when Juliet mentioned the apparition's missing feet, explaining, 'That's because he's standing on the old floor. Ever since we redid the third storey[*] and covered the old warped floor, he's been chopped off like that.'

In many ways this is a classic time-slip apparition since Julie described how she not only encountered her ghost but also

---

[*] Told you – second floor.

seemed to enter into his environment as well. The conversation with the putative spirit is more like a classic ghostly encounter though and of course it could all have been a dream – but for the corroboration of the landlord. Whatever the actual explanation, and despite staying at the Bull for several more days, Juliet did not encounter the ghost again.

In another incident from the hotel, an 1803 visitor named Arthur Shears saw his wife off to bed before attempting to blow his brains out with a pistol as a way of escaping from some outstanding debts. Continuing his run of bad luck, his aim was poor and he lingered many hours before he died. Sadly, the era of the costume worn by Juliet's visitor (not to mention his story) would seem to argue against this being a valid candidate for her ghost. Not all hauntings have easy explanations or tie in with convenient back-stories.

In a final and rather sad addendum to the tales of the Bull, in 1797 a candle was overturned into the piled straw in the stables causing a conflagration which, despite the eventual arrival of fire tenders from Witney and Bampton, completely destroyed all the outhouses around the inn. Tragically, the fire severely injured seven coach horses which had been bedded down in the stables for the night; all the animals died of their burns shortly afterwards. It is thought that the occasional sounds of terrified animals which can be heard from the rear of the building can be traced back to this awful event.

Featuring Creatures

WE VISITED OUT-OF-PLACE CATS EARLIER but there are other, even more exotic, animal encounters from across the county that we ought to mention and the most common of these is, believe it or not, the wallaby.

In an early sighting, student Greg Caswell was somewhat surprised to see a wallaby while driving along the Benson to Crowmarsh road back in August 1985 – he did attempt to pursue the animal but despite his best efforts it managed to evade him and escape into the bushes. There is a sad corollary to this encounter because a drowned wallaby, presumably the same animal, was found in a back-garden swimming pool in Crowmarsh just over a week later. Oxfordshire is a hazardous place for macropods: in early June 2002 a kangaroo or wallaby was found dead near the Stokenchurch junction of the M40. The police made attempts to trace any possible owner but without success. A spokesman commented that sightings were common around Milton Keynes, where they were assumed to be escapees from a local wildlife park, but finding one on the Oxfordshire/Buckinghamshire border clearly caught them on the hop. A similar sad little animal was found run over on the A34 south of Oxford in 2005.

These occasional sightings may seem exceptional but what are we to make of another report of a wallaby observed bounding merrily across a field near AERE Harwell in 2005? Not to mention the one which made an appearance in Henley town centre back in 1984. Even this seems fairly mundane compared to a report of a burglary made by a woman in Henley in June 2002. She called the police because a window to her basement had been broken in what looked like an attempted break-in. Blood found on the glass was sent away for analysis only to come back with the result that the donor had been a wallaby.* This incident occurred later in the month than the M40 discovery so there were clearly a number of the animals present in the county at the time. Maybe Henley is something of a marsupial-magnet. The would-be bouncing burglar was never spotted in the town so its whereabouts thereafter remain a mystery. Are all these creatures the result of a mass break-out from a wildlife park somewhere? The Cotswold Wildlife Park was clearly tired of getting the blame. 'All of our wallabies are individually identified and regularly checked. We would soon know if it was one of ours that had managed to get out,' commented a spokesman.

Again, while hardly paranormal but most definitely continuing the theme, there was much fuss in 1971 when a pelican which had escaped from Dudley Zoo took to living in gravel pits near Dorchester on Thames before being recaptured and returned home. 2015 saw a five-month-old emu called Edward escape from his enclosure in Wheatley and go, literally, on the run. The bird briefly became a twitter sensation,** generated regular police updates and even appeared in the national press. Eventually Edward (identified as female by some sources) was spotted in a field and was recaptured and reunited with his owner after five days.

There are clearly more flightless birds being kept as pets in Oxfordshire than we realise; a rhea legged it from his home on a farm near Henley in 2019. Chris*** was clearly a wiser bird than Edward as he remained free for a full five weeks before being trapped in a suburban garden, a garden fence foiling his last attempts at a rhea-guard action.

And another odd sighting, with a number of reports of an unknown creature spotted in Wytham Woods in the early 2000s. Most witnesses described it as resembling a bear: now that would be an impressive escapee. Needless to say no trace of the animal was ever actually discovered, so perhaps this is more of an spectral sighting than an actual animal encounter.

---

* Luckily the animal confined itself to the basement; presumably it realised that the rest of the house was out of bounds.
** As #RodHull.
*** What else would it be called?

FEATURING CREATURES

The Over Norton crocodile

If contemporary tales of wandering wallabies and roaming rheas aren't strange enough how about this story from the middle of the nineteenth century? In 1862 Chipping Norton landowner George Wright went to visit one of his tenants, William Phillips, at Over Norton where he noticed a small stuffed crocodile, approximately 30cm or 12 inches long, in a glass case. On enquiring where the specimen had come from, he was astonished to hear the tale that Phillips had to tell – so astonished that he wrote to *The Field* magazine and, some year later, to *The Gentleman's Magazine* about it.

Back in 1856 or 1857, while walking around the farm,

> [Phillip's] attention was attracted by the sight of, as he at first thought, a lizard, lying in the gutter, evidently but lately killed, its bowels protruding from a wound in its belly. Upon, however, taking it up, he soon discovered that the animal was not a lizard [...] he immediately asked his labourers, who were close by, if they knew anything about it. The answer was that they had killed it as it ran out of [a] stack of wood, I think the day before; and on Mr. Phillips expressing his regret at their having done so without bringing it to him alive, they replied they could easily get him another, as at the place where the wood was cut a few miles from the farm, near to Chipping Norton Common, and not far from the village of Salford, at the 'Minny' Pool* [...] they saw them frequently in the water and on the land, and often running up the trees.**

Mr Phillips promised his workmen a guinea if they could procure him another specimen but unfortunately, despite their

---

* The author speculates that 'Minny' refers to a pond with Minnows.
** Unusual behaviour for a crocodile I would think.

claims of other reptiles being seen in the area, none was ever forthcoming. Disappointed, Phillips stuffed and mounted the animal and displayed it in his home.

George Wright was able to get the great naturalist Prof. Richard Owen to examine the creature 'and he at once proclaimed the animal to be a crocodile, "not long from the egg", but would not in any way entertain the belief that the little creature had been found alive in this country.' His prime theory was that Phillips had been tricked by his farmhands although this seems unlikely since, 'the labourers who killed it would gain nothing by telling a deliberate falsehood in the matter, nor is it at all likely they would attempt the trick upon their master for no reason at all. Had they even called his attention to the dead reptile, there might have been a slight cause for suspicion; but they did nothing of the kind, and my full belief is that the creature might have remained where Mr. Phillips found it for many a long day, for any interest that the workmen in question would have taken in it.'

After being assured that the crocodile had indeed been caught in England, Owen expressed the belief that, were this the case, it could only have escaped from a touring menagerie. Later correspondents to *The Gentleman's Magazine* speculated that the animal may have hatched from a lost egg; both propositions being questionable given that the pond where the animal was found was many miles from the nearest road.

A Mr C. Parr, writing in the same publication, was able to confirm the story through an independent sighting from the 1830s.

> A person formerly resident at Chipping Norton, crossing a field [...] in company with some friends was pursued by an animal of the crocodile kind which chased them across the field situated above some waste ground known as the Common. They had some difficulty escaping from it but eventually one of the lads crushed its head with a large stone. They were afraid to touch it afterwards in case it should not be dead. The person (a woman) described it as being a foot long; and crossing near the same place some years after she saw a smaller animal of the same species. A footpath led past a pond from which the animal followed them. The pond has now been filled up for some years.'

Perhaps that is why the animal(s) moved to Over Norton.

Yet another sighting was reported in *The Field* in 1862 meaning that, for some years in the mid-nineteenth century at least, a population of possible crocodiles was living in north Oxfordshire. It must be said that George Wright had little time for the lost-from-a-menagerie theory and speculated that the alligators were part of a long-hidden indigenous population of reptiles which had managed to live undetected for many years. Given the lack of physical evidence for our black cats perhaps his theory isn't quite as outlandish as it may seem.*

Let's bring things, briefly at least, back to cats. Ed is a stonemason who specialises in the restoration of old buildings, so he was obviously a natural choice to do some repairs to the interior stonework in one of the older parts of Corpus Christi College in Oxford. It was late on a wintry, overcast afternoon as he finished his day's work and prepared to head off home. Packing away his tools he swept up the residue of dust from the block of stone with which he was working and climbed up a ladder fixed to the side of the scaffolding structure to reach the power box to switch off his powerful working lights.

As Ed reached the top of the ladder and his head rose above the level of the boards, he discovered that he was not alone: a constellation of lights, arranged in pairs, were gazing fixedly back at him. As his eyes became accustomed to the darkness at the top of the platform Ed realised that he was the undivided subject of attention of at least thirty cats, some of which were perched on the various pieces of stonework that were being refashioned and some of which were scattered randomly about the platform. But each and every cat was paying him an unnerving amount of attention; clearly his arrival was unwelcome.

Ed paused, entirely unsure what to do. He was uncomfortably aware that he was at the top of a tall ladder and singularly poorly placed to fight off one angry cat, let alone few scores of claws, but before he could even start to think about making a tactical retreat the cats, almost as one, turned and melted away into the shadows leaving him alone. Ed switched off the power and hastily retreated to ground level, collected his things and left

---

* If you think this unlikely it is worth noting that a colony of feral wild Honey Bees, of a species long thought extinct, were found alive and well on the Blenheim Palace Estate in 2021.

Corpus Christi, college of cats

the building. On his way out he stopped at the College Lodge to ask if there was a College cat. The Lodge porter confirmed that there was just one cat and was surprised to hear Ed's story since the resident moggie was notoriously territorial and renowned for chasing intruders away.

So, what could be the explanation for Ed's odd encounter? There are numerous folkloric references to weird gatherings of animals from bird tribunals to stoat funerals so large, unexpected gatherings are not entirely unprecedented. Take, for example, a report from the 1920s in which a miner returning home from work one evening came across a crowd of over fifty felines, making Ed's clowder of cats* seem restrained in comparison. Not surprisingly, the miner left the scene in some haste, doubtless feeling much the same sense of veiled threat as did Ed himself. It is a shame that Ed never tried to find out whether there was some hidden entrance that the cats might have used

---

*Yes, that *is* the correct collective term.

to gain access to the scaffold planking, nor whether anyone else had seen a cavalcade of cats either entering or leaving Corpus that day, but it is perhaps significant that he never saw another cat for the rest of the time he worked at the college. Ed was rather pleased at that since he confessed to having been rather unnerved by the whole experience. Certainly, he came away with a better understanding of why another collective noun for cats is *a glaring*.

Let's just take a trip back to 1976, staying with cats but returning to the subject of ghosts. At this time the Kerr family lived in East Oxford with their three pet cats and one evening Mr Kerr was in his back room looking out into the garden when he noticed the reflection of a cat sitting behind him. Despite having three pet cats in the household he found the way that this animal was looking at him somehow disturbing. Even so, assuming that the cat was one of his own pets, he called out and turned around only to discover that the spot where it had seemed to be sitting was entirely unoccupied. The animal would have had no chance to move in the brief time it had taken him to turn around and when he returned his gaze to the window the animal's reflection had (thankfully) also disappeared. Joining the rest of his family in the main sitting room he discovered that all the family's cats were present – and had been for some time. Had he been visited by a ghost cat? It is a shame that he didn't watch it for longer; this being Oxford I wonder if it would have faded away to just a smile.

And, to bring this diversion into the animal kingdom to a close, let's move from felines to rodents. In 1977 the guinea pig belonging to the daughter of local author John Richardson died and was, as is usually the case, buried in the garden with due family ceremony. Some weeks later, as Richardson was leaving the kitchen, he spotted a small animal out of the corner of his eye as it scurried along the hallway. It seemed too large to be a mouse. 'Although it was the right size and shape I don't say it *was* a guinea pig,' he stressed. Doubtless shaking his head to clear it, he continued on his path towards the TV when his 16-year-old daughter came into the hallway. 'Phew,' she commented, 'there's a strong smell of guinea-pig in the hall'.

Otmoor, now a marshland, nature reserve and Site of Special Scientific Interest

RiOtmoor

THE DESERTED EXPANSE OF OTMOOR was marshland until the early years of the nineteenth century and was held as common land for the folk of the surrounding villages, which made it a valuable place to graze cattle, breed geese and net wildfowl for the pot. The wetland character was maintained by regular flooding from the River Ray, but in 1815 an Act of Enclosure finally became law* and work was started on a series of banks and ditches intended to drain the marshes and convert the area to more traditional (and privately-owned) agriculture. The Act was sponsored by the larger local landowners irrespective of the harm that would be done to the local people; strangely, one of the most vocal supporters of these enclosures was the Rev. Philip Searle, Rector of Oddington, one of the Otmoor peripheral villages. As a result of this Act the course of the river was dammed, the ground drained and local people evicted, giving rise to the lament:

> The fault is great in Man or Woman
> Who steals the Goose from off a Common;
> But who can plead that man's excuse
> Who steals the Common from the Goose.

Sadly, the new raised banks of the river were rather unreliable and tended to cause flooding in other areas; not those parts owned by the Act's sponsors of course. Over the next few years local opposition festered and eventually in 1829 a group of disaffected local people, both smallholders and the dispossessed,

---

* Attempts had been made since 1801 but had been continually foiled by local opposition.

lost patience and destroyed a section of the levees, flooding the moor. Twenty-two men were prosecuted for causing this destruction but escaped punishment when they claimed that their action had been necessary to prevent damage to the property of those who owned small plots of land in the area.

Encouraged by the success of this strategy local people, led by a ringleader called John Ward of Noke, began to undertake further nocturnal acts of sabotage. Wrapped in dark cloaks with faces darkened with soot and obscured by black scarves, local men would roam the area tearing up hedges and fences and generally causing a significant amount of damage. On 6 September 1830, in a major escalation of dissent, over a thousand people joined a broad daylight procession around the moor destroying every fence and boundary that they came upon. The Berkshire Yeomanry were summoned to confront the protesters and the riot act was read, but when the crowd failed to disperse forty-one men were arrested and placed into wagons to be taken to Oxford for trial. As they were being carted away a mob attacked the escorting soldiers and all forty-one prisoners managed to escape in the confusion.

The destruction continued for a number of years with the authorities making increasingly desperate attempts to identify the ringleaders – one handbill from 1833 offers a reward of £100 and a full pardon for anyone offering information leading to the capture of anyone involved in 'Felony, Riot or Conspiracy'.

Again, a rhyme from the time went:

> *I went to Noke*
> *And nobody spoke.*
> *I went to Brill*
> *They were silent still.*
> *I went to Thame*
> *It was just the same.*
> *I went to Beckley*
> *They spoke directly.*

I am assuming that this indicates that the residents of Beckley responded in a rather more vigorous fashion than their neighbours rather than this being a slur on their reliability, a point of view supported by the fact that the only recorded incident of anyone actually informing on the rebels came from the village of Charlton.

As time passed the incidence of these incidents declined (probably encouraged by an increased presence of soldiers from the 5th Dragoon Guards permanently stationed in the area) but the right of pasturage never returned. For a while in the twentieth century Otmoor was used as a bombing range but today its essential character remains, and it is now an RSPB nature reserve.

In keeping with its remote location and turbulent history the common has a version of the wild hunt story. Back in Elizabethan times the Manor of Noke was purchased by Benedict Winchcombe, a man known for his love of the pleasures in life and hunting most of all. So keen was he that he would even, to the shock and dismay of the pious villagers, ride out to hunt on a Sunday. When 'Old Winchcombe', as he became known, eventually died he was buried in the graveyard of the village chapel. Buried but not laid to rest because his ghost still could be heard, along with his pack of hounds, continuing to enjoy his passion for hunting on the open ground late at night. Eventually the villagers grew tired of this disruptive behaviour and called in twelve priests to exorcise the haunting huntsman, which is why the sounds of the chase are no longer heard across Otmoor. Of course, the hunt may be gone but there are still reports of eerie cries of distress echoing across the deserted landscape, cries which are said to be those of men trapped and drowned in the uncharted bogs of the moor.

Otmoor may also be haunted by a most unusual phantom presence and not one which can easily be seen, only experienced in the most unpleasant of ways. While studying at Oxford in 1933, future writer and physician Arthur Guirdham visited the area during the summer and stayed overnight at an inn in Beckley before returning to Oxford to sit an exam which was scheduled for two days hence. That night he was struck by a mysterious illness. 'When I went to bed that night I began to shiver violently. My rigors were coarse and repeated and beyond my control. The springs of the bed whined continuously with the violence of my movements. My teeth chattered harshly. Even the sound of their detonation was excruciating. I felt deathly cold [...] Next day I felt shrunken with cold and horribly ill. I was jaundiced, and nauseated by the sight of food.' Guirdham called for a doctor who diagnosed a 'chill on the liver', largely due to the jaundice, but after two days the jaundice and chills had receded and Guirdham was sufficiently recovered to pass his exam with ease.

But what had so affected him? He was in no doubt. 'It was years afterwards before I knew that Otmoor was one of the last resorts of malaria in England. I could well understand it. Even in my day there was a sodden luxuriance about it. It was a pool of tropical fetor sunk in the bucolic innocence of the English countryside. I learnt that well after the Middle Ages the yellow men of Otmoor were traditional. For a couple of days I had assumed their affliction.' Otmoor was indeed infested by mosquitos and malaria well into the mid-nineteenth century but the advent of malaria treatments (due in no small part to Edward Stone who discovered aspirin and who was, for a time, curate at Charlton-on-Otmoor) had largely eradicated it by the time of Guirdham's visit. In any case, the onset of the fever was amazingly sudden and the symptoms never returned. Could Otmoor have infected the visiting student with some form of phantasmic miasma? And if him, why not others?

Well, correspondence to the *Oxford Mail* in 1976 might indicate that this wasn't just an isolated incident. In a letter to the paper Bob Bloomfield described visiting friends in Beckley before driving to Stroud, where he checked into a country hotel. That night he was seized by a fit of fierce shivering and aching muscles, unlike anything he had ever experienced before, and spent a disturbed few hours before eventually falling into a deep sleep. When he awoke he was amazed to discover that he felt entirely fit and healthy and every trace of the previous night's fever had vanished completely. All of which raises some disturbing questions. After all, if we have human phantoms, spirits of horses and even ghostly guinea pigs, then why not spectral mosquitos or malarial parasites?

Shall we return to more traditional ghost stories? The Nut Tree pub in Murcott (which takes its name from a tree which used to grow outside the pub when it opened for business during the eighteenth century) was allegedly used as a base of operations for the Otmoor Rioters and it is said that the whispered voices of the conspirators can sometimes be heard coming from the darker corners of the bar late at night.

The Nut Tree Inn, Murcott

Despite the cheerful imagery of the name the building suffered a serious fire many years ago and the young daughter of the landlord was tragically killed. In a sad reminder of this event local legend says that a girl of around eleven years of age wearing a smocked dress and flowered bonnet has been seen wandering about the pub, understandably wearing an unhappy expression on her face.

The current staff tell a slightly different tale. Mike the chef explained that the present pub had originally been three separate cottages, two of which had shared an oven – this is the area which is now behind the bar. In their version of the story a young girl had climbed into the oven to hide and the family on the other side of the shared wall had chosen that moment to light the fire to make bread. The young girl had found herself unable to open the door from inside and had perished. One can only imagine the horror when the family opened the oven door to place their dough inside.

It is assumed that the ghost which haunts the building is the spirit of that young girl. The Evans family, who ran the Nut Tree for twenty-five years were well acquainted with the ghost, so much so that they dubbed her 'Lucy', describing her as harmless but rather mischievous. As Mike puts it now: 'Lucy just likes to join in'. While her present activities are limited to occasionally moving bottles around (although one or two have been broken) she did cause a certain amount of trouble to the Evans family, especially when their children were younger. On one particular evening the children were playing happily in the sitting room of the cottage beside a roaring fire in the fireplace when Mrs Evans was horrified to notice that the fireguard was no longer in place in front of the hearth. Not unnaturally perhaps, she berated her husband for being so careless. He in return was adamant that he had put the guard in place as soon as he had lit the fire and that it had been there when he left the room.

After a moment's thought Mrs Evans decided that the only possible culprit was Lucy and told her, loudly and firmly, that she would not tolerate any more dangerous pranks. Lucy clearly felt suitably chastened: while bottles still moved around the bar the fireguard was never touched again.

Returning to Noke, where nobody spoke, the old Plough Inn (a private house since the 1990s, alas) may not (as far as we know) have hosted any rioters but it did play host to some sort of supernatural visitor for several years. In the 1980s the landlady's daughter approached an old lady dressed in a shawl (whom she assumed to be a customer) and went to pass her a menu, only for her to suddenly vanish. Other customers around the same time reported encountering the same figure.

The most unpleasant aspects of the Plough haunting seem to have centred on the toilet block to the back of the building. Visitors to the pub when it was still operating often reported an odd sense of being watched and the landlord's son was driven out of the area by what he described as an 'awful sensation' back in 1980. He also recounted hearing the sound of footsteps moving around even when there was no-one inside the out-building at the time. More disturbingly, the landlady heard the handle on one of the doors rattling one evening and, on investigating, was terrified to see the latch moving deliberately up and down as if being lifted by an unseen hand. Perhaps it is a good job that the block was demolished during the conversion to a private dwelling.

Serving Spirits

SINCE OTMOOR HAS POINTED US in this direction, let's visit a few more haunted pubs, beginning with an incident from Chipping Norton, where I was alerted to a tale from the King's Arms as told by a married couple passing through the town and staying overnight at the pub *en passant*. As they sat in the bar, up against the outside wall, the woman suddenly turned around in surprise as she had felt someone tapping firmly on her shoulder. Her sense of outrage vanished immediately when she discovered nothing behind her but a blank wall. On further investigation the couple noticed the faint outline of an old, and long bricked-up, doorway just behind where they had been sitting. Were they impeding the progress of a former regular, still impatient to reach the bar? I tried to identify the spot at which the couple had felt the ghostly contact but did not experience anything similar during my visit. I can however confirm that I did have a rather more enjoyable encounter with a couple of taps while investigating the tale.

We usually think of ghosts as being grey or white but Joe experienced a rather different apparition while visiting the Olde Swan Inn in Faringdon a few years ago. 'My girlfriend Sue and I were sitting in the Swan one lunchtime,' he explained, 'when I noticed it getting noticeably darker, as if some clouds outside had hidden the sun. At the same time I watched a dark shape starting to appear in the corner of the bar in one of the bench seating areas. It didn't look man-shaped but was more of a shapeless dark space, a sort of negative ghost I suppose.'

Joe was so surprised by what he was seeing that he could do little but stare into the amorphous anomaly for some time. Eventually it began to fade away and he shook himself out of his shock and managed to point his partner in the direction of

The Swan at Faringdon

the shape. Sadly, by this time it was singularly unimpressive. 'Looks like a shadow to me' she commented.

Joe never saw this strange apparition again and staff at the Swan were unaware that anything mysterious had ever happened in the building so this whole event remains a puzzle. Was this a ghostly cloud, a trick of the fading light or a simple hallucination? As with so many of these more recent stories, it is a shame that there were no other witnesses to corroborate and expand on the incident.

Over in Eynsham, The Railway Inn has also had its share of ghostly activity, events detailed by John Donnely in *The Clarendonian* magazine back in 1967. In that year Mr Littlechild, the then landlord of The Railway Inn, announced that he was giving up the pub because of the continued presence of a customer who had been murdered on the premises over a century before.

It seems that this haunting had begun four years previously and while there had been no actual sightings of a ghostly figure a range of strange and inconvenient events had conspired to make life unpleasant for the family. Mr Littlechild could cope with the electrical failures which led to his fridge continually switching itself off, he could even cope with the fact that over the following years the beer taps in the cellar would regularly close themselves or the pressure just fade away, but it was the constant angry rattling of the cellar doors which finally broke his nerve. 'There's no logical explanation,' he explained. 'I've got to get out [...] he's frightened the life out of me."

Sadly, the Railway Inn closed in 1976 after a suitably bizarre accident when the contents of a lorry carrying hay spontaneously caught fire as it was turning the corner opposite the pub, causing the driver to lose control and crash, seriously damaging the structure of the building. Presumably this accident also called last orders on the resident ghost.

The Fox at Denchworth is another traditional country inn with an unusual haunting; the sound of spectral women's voices speaking an oddly archaic form of English who have been heard in the bar. There have also been occasional glimpses of these ghostly gossipers, women dressed in old-fashioned conservative black clothes who scurry quickly around a corner and vanish out of sight as soon as they are spotted.

The present staff at the pub are spectrally sceptical but Amy, who worked there during the 1990s was very much a believer. 'I was in the restaurant area one evening when I turned around to see a couple of ladies I hadn't noticed before standing looking at me from across the room,' she explained. 'They looked like a couple of fairly ordinary elderly women dressed in shapeless dark clothing and leaning together as if chatting. I turned away to lay some cutlery onto the table but when I turned back they had completely disappeared. I walked across the room to peer round the corner to see if they had sat down but they were nowhere to be seen. It wasn't spooky as such, but I did think it was a bit strange.'

Originally named and styled after the traditional tree in which Charles II hid to escape his enemies as he fled after being defeated at the Battle of Worcester in 1651, the Royal Oak in Wantage was re-signed to commemorate the Royal Oak

---

* Why the poor murder victim should choose to cause mischief in in the pub in not explained. Perhaps he is just bitter.

battleship, built in 1914 and eventually torpedoed and sunk by a U-Boat torpedo at Scapa Flow in 1939.

Despite both royal and naval references in its name the Oak has a ghost of a rather different sort: a phantom dog. A number of regulars and staff have reported seeing glimpses of a small dog in a corner of the bar over the years. Paul and Frankie who run the pub own dogs themselves and dogs are welcome in the bars but the apparitional Airedale or chimeric Corgie is never spotted when any other animals are around. Its appearances are brief and once glimpsed it can never be found no matter how hard a witness may look. Could this phantom Fido be the pet of a previous landlord?

Dating back to 1642, the Crooked Billet in Stoke Row is one of those pub names which could derive from a number of sources. A billet is traditionally a military or other temporary barracks, so it is possible that the name derives from a previous use as a lodging house for soldiers, but it is more likely that the designation harks back to an older definition, that of a simple wooden stick or branch. As the use of tokens or signs to indicate the location of inns came into common usage some establishments were able to commission expensive painted or carved representations of their names; King's Heads, White Harts and Blue Boars abounded. Sadly, not every tavern was suitably grand (or profitable) enough to warrant an expensive emblem and hanging a bent stick over the door was probably sufficient to christen the Crooked Billet.

We encounter another highwayman here, this time probably the most famous of all: Dick Turpin. Turpin rented Manor Farm in Appleford for a time and so was clearly active locally, which means that there may be a modicum of truth in the rumour that Turpin romantically involved with the landlord's daughter,* a young lady by the name of Bess. Local people claim that such was his attachment to his beau that he named his famous horse, Black Bess, after her.

Whatever the truth of this assertion the pub is indubitably haunted by someone or something although, given that the haunting consists of the sound of barrels being moved around in the cellar to the accompaniment of copious swearing, I think

---

* Given his reputation there was probably little actual romance.

it is safe to assume that the resident ghost is a former member of staff rather than Turpin himself. Perhaps it is that of George Ewins, the landlord in 1865, who was charged with riotous behaviour and hauled up before a judge to defend himself. As a demonstration of his contrition Ewins declared that after his arrest he had attempted suicide by throwing himself down the well at the inn. Fortunately for him a period of drought meant that the well was empty and the worst that happened was that the hapless publican broke his ankle in the fall and was forced to spend the night at the bottom of his own well until he could be rescued. He was fined 5 shillings.

There is much debate about the origins of the name Turville but it seems likely that it derives from the Anglo-Saxon *ther-field* meaning open field. Over time the village has been recorded as Thyrefeld in 1240, Turfeld in 1445, and Turfield in 1766. The first documented record of the present Turville is in 1826 and it is presumed that the 'ville' suffix shares a root with the Dutch/Germanic veldt, also meaning open fields.* Were there settlers from the Low Countries in the area around this time who profoundly influenced the local lexicon?

Whatever the origins of the village name itself the origin of the pub name, the Bull and Butcher, should be fairly obvious surely? Apparently not. According to the pub itself, the name has little to do with the meat trade and everything to do with Tudor politics, an explanation that relies heavily on the spelling on the crest of Sir Thomas Bullen, father of the second of Henry VIII's wives, Anne Boleyn. (It is thought that the spelling was 'gentrified' after Anne had acted as a lady-in-waiting at Margaret of Austria's court in Mechelen and, later, to the French Queen Consort, Queen Claude. At this point the family name is recorded as Boleyne so it is easy to see how the more usually accepted modern spelling came into use.) In any case, it is proposed that the pub name refers to The Bullen Butcher, clearly a reference to Anne's execution by her husband the King. Now, I like a pun as much as anyone but even to me this seems something of a stretch, especially as the inn was not granted a license until 1617, supposedly after workmen building the village church went on strike because of the lack of local refreshments.

---

* Although the simple French ville (town) is also an option.

The Bull and Butcher was the scene of a tragic murder in 1942 when the landlord, Lacey Beckett, took a shotgun into the family bedroom and shot both his wife and dog dead in cold blood and then decamped to the pub orchard (now the car park) and killed himself. There were rumours in the village that his wife had been having an affair with the local blacksmith so this may have been the motive behind the murder, but it seems a little unfair to include the poor dog in this bloody revenge.

Neither of the tragic figures in this story seems to have been able to move on.[*] Beckett's ghostly figure has been glimpsed in the pub late at night and the sound of rolling barrels can sometimes be heard echoing up from the cellar – although nothing is ever found to have been moved when staff summon up the courage to go down to investigate. Mrs Beckett has also been glimpsed, dressed in a simple brown dress and, perhaps unsurprisingly, crying inconsolably.

Moving to Oxford, the odd name of The Eagle and Child comes from the crest of the Earl of Derby and relates to the story of a member of the family who fathered an illegitimate child and supposedly hid the baby away in the nest of an eagle only to 'coincidentally' stumble upon it, declare it an act of God, and promptly adopt the child. The pub was a favourite of the antiquarian Anthony Wood – although since he documented and claimed to have personally visited all 378 alehouses, taverns and inns in Oxford I'm not sure how he found the time to have a local. The Bird and Baby, to give the pub its local nickname, is a famous literary watering hole, most notable as the location of the gathering of the group known as the Inklings in the space known as the Rabbit Room: J. R. R. Tolkein, C. S. Lewis, Roger Lancelyn Green, Charles Williams and others. Obviously such a concentration of fantastical imagination has seeped into the fabric of the building because it has developed a ghost all of its own although, as one might expect, it is a fairly civilised example of the species.

Some years ago, the then landlord went down into the cellar to change a barrel of beer. The pub had closed for the night so everything was quietly subdued in the way only a pub after closing can manage. As he wrestled with the pipes the landlord caught sight of a woman standing quietly off to one side watching him

---

[*] Clearly the dog was far luckier in that respect.

The Eagle and Child, Oxford

struggle. Assuming that it was his wife coming to offer a hand, he finished up his task and looked up to speak to her only to discover that he was alone. He was about to call upstairs to ask why she had disappeared in such a hurry when he realised that he had neither heard anyone coming down into the cellar, nor anyone leaving. Needless to say, from that time onwards he always insisted on having company whenever he had to descend into what had evidently become an uncomfortable working environment.

So, who was this mysterious woman? There were no women in the Inklings so we cannot create a literary connection (unless we call up the shade of Amanda McKittrick Ros – not a local author but an Irish writer whose work the Inklings took endless delight in disparaging – or Dorothy L. Sayers who was peripherally associated with the group) so, as in so many cases, we will just have to assume that the spirit was a former member of staff keeping a professionally watchful eye on the premises. One potential suspect might be Florence Blagrove who was landlady for 40 years and who kept pet rabbits in the eponymous room. If she is the spirit of the inn then she has stayed on long after her own closing time.

The Jolly Tucker in Witney gained its name because it was the favoured drinking establishment of the weavers and tuckers* who worked in the town's famous blanket industry

---
* Weavers produced the blankets while the tuckers applied the finishing touches to ensure that the cloth did not come unravelled.

(sometimes the pub is referred to as the Jolly Weaver). It was one of the locations used to host the annual 'Tuckers' Feast' in the town. Tuckers' Feasts began in the early days of the woollen industry, back in the days when weaving was subcontracted out to small cottage industry weavers who would host celebratory feasts to which the master weavers of the locale would be invited. These were originally held in May and November and served as an opportunity for the workmen to claim their payment for the work that they had done over the previous six months, hence their alternative name – the Tuckers' Reckoning Feasts. With the gradual industrialisation of the blanket-making process the emphasis of the feasts switched entirely around and they became an opportunity for the mill-owner to hold a celebration as a thank you to his workers. The Tuckers' Feast is still celebrated in Witney although no longer on the traditional Shrove Tuesday.

Sadly, the Jolly Tucker is no more having been split up and converted to a fishmongers and confectioners shop in 1911, before eventually becoming a post office sometime in the 1990s. Even the post office is no more; it is now a private house, although one with perhaps just a trace of its former owners still in residence since the young wife of one of the former landlords is said to climb the staircase to the first floor. This is no shy, wallflower of a spectre; back in the 1940s the lady owner of the house* would reportedly pass the ghost on the stairs and address her casually as they passed. We can only admire her sang froid.

Some pubs may have simple hauntings but others such as The Angel Inn, also in Witney, have a far more physical supernatural story to tell: in this case, a cursed stool.

The story dates back to the beginning of the nineteenth century when one of the regular drinkers at the pub was the local lothario, a gentleman** known as Albert. Despite being a married man Albert had an eye for the local ladies and sufficient charm to be able to inveigle his way into their affections – and their beds. However, when he became smitten by the wife

---

* Some versions of the tale assert that the witness was a landlady from when the building was still a pub.
** Or not ...

The Angel Inn, Witney

of a local preacher it was a romance too far, and one which eventually ended in disaster.

One evening, presumably while the preacher was out dispensing hellfire and damnation to his flock, Albert and the lady were enjoying a little romantic interlude when they were horrified to hear the husband arrive home earlier than expected. As the preacher climbed the stairs Albert hurled himself out of the bedroom window in his haste to escape and doubtless considered himself fortunate when his fall was broken by a heap of manure which sat directly below the window. Seeing the outraged face of the cuckolded husband staring down at him from above Albert scurried away, doubtless attempting to hide both his identity and his modesty, and sought refuge in the snug of The Angel. Undeterred the preacher followed.

Safe in the dim light of the inn Albert may have considered himself suitably anonymous but the reek of the manure was to be his undoing and the angry husband quickly identified him, lashing out and catapulting him from his stool. Unfortunately, such was the strength of the blow that Albert's head struck the corner of the bar and cracked his skull. With his dying breath

Albert is said to have cursed the stool upon which had been sitting and all those who should sit upon it in future.

In folklore the curse of a dying man is a powerful thing and four people who foolishly disregarded the warnings of the Angel's regulars and sat upon the stool did indeed meet early deaths. Such was the evil reputation that the stool developed that it was removed in 1847, although whether it was placed in storage or destroyed is unknown. Possibly it is sitting in some dusty corner of an attic somewhere, just biding its time until it can be rescued by an antique hunter and returned to the world to continue its cursèd work. Coming soon to a daytime antiques show near you ...

Many years ago Banbury was particularly renowned (I kid you not) for the quality of its cheese* but less so for the quality of its local tinkers: 'Like Banbury tinkers, that in mending one hole make three'.

It also had something of a reputation for quality ales, an opinion that the staff at The Cromwell would strongly support today. The Cromwell is not generally known for being haunted but it has in fact been the scene of all sorts of odd events. 'Old buildings creak at night, it's nothing special,' Chris told me from the reception desk, 'and lights sometimes flicker, it's probably an electrical problem'. The pub, a coaching inn dating back to the 1600s and taking its name from the civil war occupation of the town, is certainly the kind of building which *would* creak – but he was clearly trying very hard to convince himself that such things had no more than a mundane explanation.

Since he has already experienced several inexplicable phenomena at the hotel it seems unlikely that he will be successful. Late one evening he spotted a strange white mist on the CCTV camera pointed along the corridor leading from the bar to the rear garden. Unnerved, especially as he was the only member of staff on the premises at the time, he cautiously went to investigate only to discover that the area was entirely fog free, clear of cloudiness and any mist was entirely missing. Returning to his post he was relieved to see that the camera view was once again normal but, when he reviewed the footage the cloud he had noticed before was clearly visible. The camera

---

* In *The Merry Wives of Windsor* Shakespeare has Bardolph call Abraham Slender a 'Banbury Cheese' as a compliment.

recordings are motion-activated so there had clearly been ... something ... in the corridor that night but he was unable to suggest what it might have been. Unfortunately, he did not think to save the CCTV footage.

As if this wasn't enough Chris was down in the beer cellars one night when the lights began to flicker and suddenly went out plunging the area into almost total darkness. Feeling somewhat uneasy Chris began to edge his way towards the stairs, at which point something tapped him firmly on the shoulder. 'I have never run so fast in my life,' he admitted.

The haunted passageway at the Cromwell, where the ecto-mist was seen on CCTV

Lincoln College Library and Rector's Lodgings

Oxford's Most Haunted College

WHILE THERE ARE MANY COLLEGES which can boast historical ghost stories one Oxford college seems to be the locus of far more recent paranormal activity. Welcome to Lincoln: Oxford's most haunted College.

Actually, Lincoln does have an historical ghost story. During the Civil War, while Oxford was a Royalist stronghold and the courts of both King Charles and Queen Henrietta were based in the city, the colleges were not only called upon to surrender their dining silver to support the King's cause but were also drafted in to perform more practical tasks to aid the war effort. And so it was that Lincoln found itself required to securely host a group of Parliamentary soldiers who had been captured during a skirmish nearby. Having nowhere particularly secure to keep the men, they were unceremoniously ushered into a cellar and locked into the darkness. Needless to say this was not a particularly hygienic environment in which to keep so many men and they quickly succumbed to some sort of prison fever and died. It is said that their spirits haunt the cellar to this very day.* It is a colourful legend but sadly none of the college histories mention the event so it may well be entirely apocryphal.

---

* On a personal note, I was once locked in this very cellar when the trap door closed and jammed. In the hour I spent trapped in the darkness I cannot say that I can confirm the existence of the phantom parliamentarians; I can however confirm the existence of any number of rats ... A previous Bursar, whose office sits directly above the haunted space, once reported hearing banging coming from the cellar but I suspect that may have been me trying to attract attention. Or a ghostly re-enactment thereof.

In any case it is more recent hauntings that interest us here. There were, for many years, rumours of sightings of the ghost of the late wife of Rector Montgomery on one of the staircases. Mrs Montgomery had been interred in the College gardens but, following renovations, her remains were moved and she has certainly not made her presence felt since then.

The Rector of Lincoln is the title given to the College Head of House, the equivalent of the Principal or Warden in many other colleges.* The Rector lives in a nineteenth-century property built on the college grounds, a sprawling building over three floors and, crucially, possessing a spacious set of basement rooms. In the 2000s one of these cellars was the source for the electrical power cabling to the house and so various members of the maintenance staff would occasionally have to undertake work in the area. Late one autumn afternoon, one of the electricians ventured downstairs to do some standard safety checks on the fuseboard. As he finished his work and bent to pick up his tool bag he was pushed firmly from behind and stumbled forward, almost falling over. Supposing that someone else had crept into the basement behind him he turned angrily around, only to discover that he was alone. Far from hearing retreating footsteps, and perhaps laughter, the only sound to be heard was the buzzing of the wires. Suddenly realising that he was alone in a cellar – yet not alone – he hastily retreated upstairs and refused, from that day onwards, to work in the basement on his own. This area is now used as a boiler room; clearly the constant humming and thrumming is not conducive to supernatural shoving as staff have not recorded any odd occurrences since.

While the Mitre, located at the end of Turl Street adjacent to the College, is first recorded as a tavern in 1300, the present building was built around 1630, with a rather younger frontage dating back to the eighteenth century. Parts of the site, especially sections of the cellars, may even have been constructed as far back as Saxon times. The inn's name comes from the main part of the Mitre being acquired in 1488 by Lincoln College. Lincoln was founded in 1427 by the Bishop

---

* The title is a hangover from the time when the university was basically a collection of theological colleges.

of Lincoln, the bishop's symbol of office (and the College crest) being the bishop's tall headpiece, the mitre. Amusingly, the building was locally known as The Cardinal's Hat for a time.

The fabulous barrel-vaulted cellar bar (sadly now a storeroom) dates back to the fourteenth century and is remembered by German Pastor C. P. Moritz, whose eighteenth-century journey across England, undertaken entirely on foot, is recorded in his *Travels Through Several Parts of England* (1782). According to Moritz, as he wearily approached Oxford he was overtaken by a don returning from his Dorchester curacy. Being educated men they conversed in Latin for a while until they reached the city. The English priest was unfailingly hospitable and, even though he was plainly exhausted from his travels, insisted on introducing Moritz to several other Oxford worthies. Moritz and his new friends spent the evening drinking heavily and Moritz reported spending most of the next day in bed with an appalling hangover from the 'copious and numerous toasts of my jolly and reverend friends'.

But I digress. Again. The rooms above and behind the restaurant, which would once have housed guests at the inn during its heyday, are now used as student accommodation by the college. There have long been tales told of phantom footsteps roaming the echoing corridors late at night but, more frighteningly, one of the scouts (cleaners) who was making up an unused student room some years ago was also forcibly pushed from behind by something unseen and found herself sprawled face-first across the bed she was attempting to change. Struggling to her feet she too looked around but there was, of course, no-one in sight. These rooms are just across Turl Street from the Rector's Lodgings basement; could this be the same ectoplasmic entity which was active there? Certainly the *modus operandi* is similar.* This part of the building has just been extensively renovated and is now used both for students during term and as a hotel at other times, so it will be interesting to see if this encourages or supresses such activity in future.

Occupying the space at the end of Turl Street between the Mitre and the Rector's Lodgings is the church of St Mary and

---

* It is a scary thought that there might be a peripatetic poltergeist roaming up and down Turl Street: where might it appear next?

All Saints. This was originally the parish church for this part of Oxford and the annual beating of the bounds ceremony (and the throwing of coins to children from the college tower) on Ascension Day each year, reflect this fact. However, the church was decommissioned in the 1970s and is now the college library. The bodies interred in the crypt downstairs were relocated and reburied during the renovation, and the space below ground level is now a separate library reading room and boiler/maintenance space.

While the removal of the bodies was done with all due ceremony it is possible that someone, or something, was unhappy with the new arrangements because after the redevelopment the scout assigned to the library experienced a number of unexplained incidents. Despite being a meticulous person, each morning she would find her cleaning equipment and supplies, all kept in the redeveloped area of the old crypt, disturbed and moved around in the store cupboard. Sometimes, books from the shelves would be found lying on the library floor although, interestingly, never damaged and lying as if they had been placed there rather than fallen or been thrown from the shelves. The library is locked at night, so the possibility of a student

The college library at night, under a full moon

prank seems unlikely. Luckily, after some months the activity became less frequent and eventually stopped completely.

And a final tale from just a year or two ago. An American student, part of a summer school programme staying at Lincoln, had been allocated one of the older bedrooms in college up in the eaves at the top of a narrow and winding staircase. She was ecstatic to have been given this room and was extremely happy there – until one night she was woken by a crash from her en-suite bathroom area. Switching on the light she opened the door to discover that the contents of a glass shelf on the wall had been swept aside and into the sink below. Clearly no-one could have got into her room and the shelf was undamaged so there was no rational explanation as to what had caused the toiletries to end up in the sink. As you might expect, she did not switch off the light that night; nor for the remainder of her stay ...

Across the High Street from The Mitre sits The Chequers whose name and distinctive inn sign arises because from its earliest days (the pub claims 1260) until 1434 the building served as the headquarters of a moneylender; a profession which took a chequered board as its symbol. All Souls College purchased the property in 1466, and it was later rebuilt as a tavern by Alderman Richard Kent in about 1500, whereupon it became known as Kent's Hall. The earliest reference to the Chequers name dates from 1605 when a draper named John Greene was issued a licence to brew and sell ale on the premises.

The various landlords of the Chequers were clearly eager to stand out among the crowded tavern scene in Oxford and the building was the scene of a number of locally famous 'displays' over the years including, in 1757, a camel from Egypt and, the following year, a pair of conjoined twins. Clearly the lure of the exotic was a profitable enterprise and by 1762 the inn was able to offer a small menagerie to visitors including a sea-lion, a racoon and a large fish which may well have been a shark. Not forgetting the draw of their earlier human visitors, the inn also played host to a giant from Herefordshire in 1776; such was his popularity that he was reputed to have been regularly spirited away to dine at the various colleges around the city.

You may be wondering why I am discussing the Chequers at

this point. Well, of course, given such a chequered* history, it is obvious that the pub has its own claim to spectral inhabitants. In this case the story is that during the dissolution of the monasteries a group of protesting monks were rounded up and driven into the underground passages which criss-cross the High Street and sealed in the darkness to starve. It is said that their screams can still be faintly heard late at night when the inn and the town around it are dark and quiet. The purported tunnel leads directly from the cellars of the Chequers to the underground vaults beneath the Mitre. Are the hauntings related?

According to landlady Kerry the staff at The Chequers are well aware that they are supposed to have a resident ghost or two but have never encountered any of their moaning monks in person, although one patron did report catching a fleeting glimpse of a cowled figure in the upper restaurant area of the building, hard up against the fifteenth-century altar screen which adorns the far wall.

During major renovation work some years ago a child's shoe was discovered behind a fireplace and removed, the intention being that it would go on display somewhere in the building. You may not be surprised to discover that the removal of the shoe led to a spate of sightings of a young girl around the building and an outbreak of minor poltergeist activity, with objects disappearing and rematerialising in unexpected places. After some weeks of enduring this trivial but annoying behaviour the shoe was returned to its original hiding place, and the activity stopped as suddenly as it had started.

---

* Sorry.

Witches, Wizards and Wise Folk

WE TOUCHED ON THE TOPIC of witches when we visited the Rollright Stones but there are a surprising number of tales of witches, and their cousins the wizards and cunning people, right across the county. More witches than you can shake a broomstick at in fact.

William Monk, writing in his *History of Witney* in 1894, claimed that there had been at least two active witches during the time of the Napoleonic wars who 'were generally supposed to have had commerce with the evil one'.* In an echo of a common legend, it was said that at least one of the women was in the habit of transforming herself into the form of a hare and roaming about the district causing mischief. A local farmer shot at a hare on his land one night, wounding it in the leg, and that woman had been mysteriously lame ever since.

Alfred Beesley's *History of Banbury* tells the tale of an ancient ash tree which grew atop Barrow Hill, an ancient burial mound just outside the village of Sulgrave, which was used as a gathering place for the local coven. Being unwilling to host this kind of company the villagers decided to chop down and burn the tree** in the hope that the witches would take their coven elsewhere. However, understandably unwilling to be driven away, the witches cast a great illusion and as the villagers marched on the hill they looked back towards their homes to see flames and smoke engulfing them. Rushing back to douse the flames the tree was forgotten, and the witches were able to remain. Of course, why the people of Sulgrave did not return

---

* I assume he meant Satan rather than Napoleon.
** Ashes to ashes?

The barrow at Sulgrave

even more enraged at having been tricked is never explained. Presumably they took this as a warning that the next fire might be real.

Witches obviously have an affinity for ash trees. Another famous ancient example stood at Wardington during the Civil War; King Charles was said to have dined beneath it before the Battle of Cropredy Bridge in 1644. The tree was another gathering place for a local coven who would dance around it at midnight, but it died at the end of the eighteenth century, and they drifted away elsewhere. Possibly to Sulgrave I suppose. The ash was replaced and a tree stands on the spot to this day.

One of a witch's powers is that of foretelling the future and when Farmer Felix Maggs went to visit one, unnamed, wise woman in South Moreton in 1894 he will have been surprised at the specific nature of her prediction: he was destined to be 'struck down by a great black horse'. Thus warned he took great care to avoid contact with scary stallions and frightening fillies, so will have been somewhat surprised to be run down and killed by a train a few years later. Never take the advice of a witch at face value: Maggs was killed by an irony horse.

Back in the nineteenth century Kirtlington was home to a notorious witch named Sarey Bowers. She was considered something of a terror in the village and any adult or child who crossed her would be sure to come to some misfortune shortly afterwards. She lived in an old hut at the top of the village called Fox Town's End because this was the point at which the village hunt would meet. In fact, while the hunt often set out from here, they met with remarkably little success and it was generally assumed that 'Old Sarey' had somehow helped the foxes and hindered the hounds in the chase. One day the hunt very nearly caught their prey but at the last minute the animal slipped into Sarey Bowers' cottage. When the huntsmen went to the door to chase it out again only Sarey could be found within, which naturally led to a rumour that she could transform herself to and from the form of a fox.

In a similar vein, back around the mid-nineteenth century in the hamlet of Newnham Murren,* local people were frightened by the apparition of a white cat late at night which was said to be the shape-shifted form of an old village woman by the name of Mother Frewin. Clearly sighting the animal became associated with bad luck as locals soon adopted the saying 'Don't stay out late, or you'll see the white cat.'

Sarey Bowers may, in reality, have just been a grouchy old lady, but in the 1890s a 91-year-old woman named Mrs Cooper from Barton in Oxford reminisced that when she had been a child Headington had been home to a genuine witch called Miriam Russell. In this case there was no doubt that Miriam was a witch as she was often to be seen riding about the area in a dough-cover – a type of container used for kneading dough.** One day Miriam went to the home of a family named Powell, who lived at Stowford Farm, to ask a favour and, when they turned her away she made a sinister statement: she would 'remember them'. A few days later, the cows and calves on the farm all started acting wildly and rushing mindlessly backwards and forwards and several calves disappeared, only to be found on the roof of the thatched barn. 'Old Miriam' made it known to the Powells that this was her work and, after they had given

---
* Now part of Crowmarsh Gifford, near Wallingford.
** Ours is not to reason why.

her whatever favour she had previously demanded, the cattle once more became quiet and the calves allowed themselves to be brought back down to the ground. Miriam was clearly a witch of both power and malice although, curiously, she was said to love children. Perhaps it was this last redeeming feature which meant that she could be buried in Headington churchyard when she died in 1845.

A similar story is told in Tetsworth, near Thame, about an old lady known as Mother Buckland. This unfortunate woman scraped by on the proceeds of begging but seems to have been able to offer a little supernatural encouragement to help her neighbours' generosity along. One day she called at a house where a woman called Phoebe Hawes was hanging out a shawl to dry. Taking a fancy to the garment Mother Buckland asked if she could have it and, on being refused, responded, ominously 'Look out! You'll know; look out!' Shortly after this exchange Mrs Hawes became increasingly confused and unwell until the old lady returned and once again asked for the shawl. This time the family were more than happy to hand it over and Mrs Hawes almost immediately began to recover. A genuine curse or the stress of thinking oneself cursed? I wonder if there is a difference.

The Rollright Witch may have transformed herself into a tree after her actions but, as we have seen, some of her crafty sisters from the area clearly decided to take a more prolonged, if somewhat malign, role in local affairs. Another such was Dolly Henderson who lived in the village of Salford at the end of the nineteenth century. A woman of the village named Ann Hulver somehow managed to offend Dolly who promptly cursed her causing her to fall ill. Ann consulted a local cunning man named William 'Wizard' Manning[*] who told her that Dolly had been the cause of her illness but that he could not cure her if she told anyone else about this. Sadly, Ann was something of a gossip and confided all this to a friend – and thus the curse continued until she was reduced to little more than skin and bones.

---

[*] Manning's primary diagnostic technique involved examining the urine of a victim for bubbles, hence he is often referred to as a water-doctor. Was he a genuine wizard or just a quack taking the ...?

WITCHES, WIZARDS AND WISE FOLK

Around the same time a young boy was also bewitched by Dolly, but when he became ill his brother angrily threw a thorny stick at the old woman. This cut her arm and she bled profusely, the flowing blood breaking both spells; Ann and the young boy recovered while the curses rebounded upon Dolly who died shortly afterwards, much to the relief of her neighbours.

The vulnerability of witches to scratching recurs in the case of 'Shaking Charlotte', a very old woman from North Leigh from around the 1800s. It was well known locally that she was a witch, and everyone also knew that her spells could be broken by scratching her or piercing her skin with a pin to draw blood. All well and good, but unfortunately everyone was too scared of her to approach and make the attempt. Charlotte was one of a community of gypsies who lived on the nearby common (probably on the part of the common known as Witches Ground) and when her husband died a huge funeral was held to cremate him, along with all his belongings, on a massive funeral pyre. After this ceremony the gypsies moved on and one man, poking around in the ashes, uncovered a half-burnt book which he took home to read. Finding it full of what he later described as 'horrible old spells' he threw the book into his own hearth to be finally consumed by the flames.

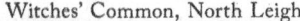

Witches' Common, North Leigh

Next up in our, surprisingly large, list of witchy women (yes, despite the brief appearance of Manning they do all seem to be women) is Betty Cann who lived in Stanton St. John in the 1820s. Betty also had a fearsome reputation and would make odd demands of workmen during harvest-time and if they disobeyed her commands some sort of misfortune would always befall them. Betty seems to have been possessed of something of the second sight as she would always know where the young people of the village had been the night before ... and what time they had finally arrived home. No wonder children were said to have been afraid to pass by her cottage. Her abilities do make me wonder whether her strange commands were more in the nature of helpful warnings of misfortunes to come and ways to avoid them, which would very much put her in the white witch category. Although, she too seems to have had the ability to cause the village cows to run madly up and down the high street and there were tales that when men of the village peered through the keyhole of her cottage they could see her dancing – with her chairs joining in. Of course, the same men also claimed that she rode around the village on a clothes horse so their reliability as witnesses may be a little suspect.

Not all witchcraft stories are rooted in folklore: some are published in the papers. In this case *Jackson's Oxford Journal* in September 1869. According to the newspaper report a young married Deddington woman, who was already in somewhat poor health, had suddenly seen her condition worsen, leading her to make strange pronouncements and utter 'horrid ravings', and at regular times between (for some reason) 8am and 4pm, suffering convulsions. Unable to determine any physical cause for her complaint doctors were nonplussed but local people quickly concluded that she had been bewitched by a local, semi-itinerant, tinker-woman.

The townsfolk offered the suffering woman an assortment of folk-remedies but to no avail and eventually a rumour started that a 'clever man' would be coming to the village the following Monday to cure the woman. According to the rapidly spreading gossip, he was planning to place straw crosses across the bewitched woman's doorstep and bend the poor tinker across the threshold – whereupon a cat would magically appear, be shot by a local man and this would effect a cure.

By the time Monday arrived Deddington was in a frenzy of anticipation. Sadly, it seems that the cunning man had business elsewhere (as we can assume did the lady tinker) but crowds assembled nonetheless both inside and outside the house. Some took to drink to calm their feverish nerves. After an evening of little event the occasion was saved when, just before 10pm, 'a most unearthly noise seemed to proceed from under the chairs and tables, enough to shake the strongest nerves.' This seems to have lasted around 15 minutes, after which the afflicted woman went into a fit.

Sadly, there is no follow-up to this story so I think we can assume that the poor woman's final convulsions brought the saga to an end. Did the spectacle of the evening banish her magical malady? Did the actions of the crowd provide the perfect placebo? Or was this simply the case of an illness which had reached its natural end?

Not all these stories of witches and cunning folk involve malice. When The Carpenters Arms in Newlands, near Eynsham, was broken into one Saturday night in March 1840 the thief made away with a locked box containing the funds of the local Benefit Society (the not-inconsiderable sum of £9) not to mention all the records of income and expenditure for the society. The landlord Swanley Poulton had actually been downstairs with his wife while the daring theft had taken place. They had heard noises coming from upstairs but had failed to investigate, so it was only later when they retired to bed that they discovered someone had made a hole in the thatched roof and climbed down into the pub to perform the robbery.

A hasty meeting of the Society was convened and a decision was made: not to call the authorities but to consult a cunning man! Poulton and two other senior members of the society rode a wagon to Adderbury where they met with this (sadly unidentified) wise person who promised that they would be reunited with their stolen property within three days. And so it proved. Well almost, for the box and the paperwork were indeed discovered a few days later: the cash, alas, was gone.

Sometimes being a cunning person brought problems with the law. Magistrates Court records for February 1864 show that 'an old woman named Mary Lobes of rather lady-like appearance and exceeding well spoken' (*Jackson's Oxford Journal* also described her as a 'respectable sorceress') was brought to court accused of telling false fortunes and plying the trade of a wise woman. Lobes had based herself in the Prince of Wales Inn at Abingdon and while her advertisements in the local press had proclaimed her a guitar teacher she had in fact been offering card readings. In one case mentioned, a couple named George and Jane Mayo had been accused by their neighbours of stealing clothes from a local man named Charles Preston at Shippon. They approached Lobes who read her cards and announced that the thief had been a dark man and the couple were therefore vindicated. It was subsequently revealed that Lobes herself may have started the rumour of their guilt in the first place, presumably as a lure for their business.

Whatever the ins and outs of the case Mary Lobes denied ever telling fortunes, although she did admit to doing card readings for clients. Both she and a number of witnesses declared that she took no money for these readings, but the Bench still found her guilty of the charge. However, since she had already spent some time awaiting trial they set her punishment at just one more day in prison, on the understanding that her next offence would carry a sentence of a full three months. One can only wonder if her treatment would have been different had she been somewhat less 'respectable'.

And finally, a reminder that not all witchy-women dabble in the *dark* arts; some come from a more formal religious background. Elizabeth Poole was born sometime after 1620 in London and when she was about sixteen she joined a radical protestant sect known as the Particular Baptists led by William Kiffin. Her membership of the church lasted for 20 years but she was eventually expelled for 'heresy and immorality', and subsequently moved to Abingdon* where she was befriended by Thomasine Pendarves, wife of John Pendarves, a local Baptist minister.

She briefly came to prominence in December 1648 (in the early, turbulent years of the post-Civil War Commonwealth) when she spoke at a plenary session of the Council of army officers. She related details of a vision she had experienced

---

* It is possible that she had followed a Parliamentary soldier and lover, hence the accusation of immorality.

in which the army (in the form of a healthy young man) cured the nation (manifesting as a sick woman) of a crippling disease. The power to do this, she explained, came directly from God working through the Parliamentary forces. This odd pronouncement seems to have been part of a strategy to try to foster some sort of unity between the Parliamentary army and the more extreme puritan Leveller movement to which she belonged. Sadly, no accord between the two sides was ever reached (a problem which plagued the Commonwealth throughout its existence) but when details of her vision became more widely known Poole acquired the title of *The Prophetess of Abingdon*. Of course, whether her vision was a divine sending, mystical vision or cynical political ploy is an open question.

Shortly afterwards, on 5 January 1649, she once again appeared before the Council, this time in an attempt to intervene in the debate on whether or not the King should be executed. Arguing for clemency she declared that dire supernatural consequences would ensue should Charles be killed. The Council were clearly happy to hear prophecies which confirmed their own divine mission but were less than keen on hearing contrary opinions; when the King subsequently lost his head on 30 January and no calamities immediately befell the realm Poole lost much of her credibility and largely retreated from public political activity.

She did however publish two pamphlets titled *Alarum of War* and *Another Alarum of War*, which contained her own words as well as sections by other writers, including her mentor Thomasine Pendarves. In these she attributed her prophetic powers to 'the babe Jesus in me', clearly disassociating herself from our more common-or-garden witches. She also dramatically foresaw the punishment of the politicians who had ignored her message: 'I have seen your carcases slain upon the ground' she wrote, an accurate description of the ultimate fate of at least some of those who had signed Charles's warrant of execution.

Sadly, Elizabeth Poole mostly vanishes from history after this (although she reappears briefly when imprisoned in the Gatehouse prison in 1668 for having an unlicensed printing press at her house in Southwark) so her ultimate fate is unknown. It is nice though to be able to present a story of a woman using her (possibly) supernatural gifts for a lofty political purpose. With not a badly-behaved bovine to be seen.

Pope's Tower, Stanton Harcourt

Pond Memories

We skipped lightly over the idea of laying ghosts in ponds at Bampton and Stanton Harcourt in an earlier chapter to concentrate on barrels. Now would seem a good time to redress the balance and revisit this theme, and indeed, Stanton Harcourt itself.*

The original manor house here was mostly demolished in the mid-eighteenth century, but the remaining structure (including the fourteenth-century Great Kitchen) was extensively rebuilt in the nineteenth century and can be seen as the manor house today. Our tale however concerns the fifteenth-century tower which stands in the grounds, and which has gone by the name of Pope's Tower since the poet Alexander Pope stayed in the upper rooms in 1717–18. It is however a far more tragic inhabitant of the tower which concerns us: Lady Alice Harcourt.

Her story is a sad one, for Lady Alice was supposedly murdered in one of the rooms on the first floor of the tower. While her family went off to mass her killer dismembered her body and disposed of the parts by throwing them out of the small window. Neither the most efficient nor the cleanest way of disposing of a body I would suggest. It is said that her (miraculously intact) ghost was unable to find peace and could frequently be seen in both the tower and the manor garden, and so her spirit was banished to one of the nearby ponds by a party of priests. When the weather is hot and the pond dries out her ghost is allegedly freed to walk the grounds

---

* In for a penny, in for a pond?

once more. The pond in which her ghost rests[*] is still known as Lady Alice's Pond.

There is another, confusingly similar, legend from the manor which relates how a young girl, having been jilted by her lover, drowned herself in the pond. Presumably this is a less violent, or more romanticised, version of Lady Alice's tale as this shade was also laid by a collection of clerics in the pond, and also walks when the pond dries. As a nod to an earlier section of this book, she sometimes also drives a coach and horses around the grounds, a post-mortem hobby which would suggest that whoever the ghost may be, she was not one of the serving staff at the manor.

Pope himself tells a different story about the tower. He describes being shown around by the house steward who 'led us up the tower by dark winding stone steps, which landed us into several little rooms one above another. One of these was nailed up, and our guide whispered to us as a secret the occasion of it: it seems the course of this noble blood was a little interrupted about two centuries ago, by a freak of the Lady Frances, who was here taken in the fact with a neighbouring Prior, ever since which the room has been nailed up, and branded with the name of the Adultery-Chamber.'

Writing in a letter to the Duke of Buckingham in 1818 towards the end of his stay, Pope averred that the ghost of Lady Frances was sometimes seen in the tower, and that some of the family maids reported that they had peered through the keyhole and seen a lady wearing a farthingale 'but this matter is hushed up, and the servants forbidden to talk of it'.

There is an intriguingly brief tale from Wilcote of an unidentified 'spirit' which haunted the village and which was eventually banished by throwing the church bell, minus its clapper, into one of the village ponds. The clapper itself was consigned to another pond and the spirit was thus subdued. Rather than the ponds drying out it is claimed that the spirit is constrained until the clapper and bell are reunited. Given the trouble (and expense) of this method it seems strange that we have no more details about the ghost; it must have been impressively scary to have warranted such an extravagant exorcism.

---

[*] Or fails to rest.

In the early 1800s the son of Squire Reade of Ipsden fell in love with one of the girls in the village. As might be expected his parents disapproved of the match, it being unthinkable that a member of the gentry should be married to one of the common folk, and they forbade their son from having any contact with the young girl. Either in protest, or just from a general desire to escape the controlling grasp of his family, the young man left home and joined the army. Clearly he secretly kept in touch with his sweetheart because when he was killed a few years later she died of a broken heart. The ghost of the soldier was sometimes seen in the village (with his head tucked, unnervingly, under his arm), as was the shade of the young village girl. Presumably the headless hussar faded away more quickly that the lovelorn lass because it is her spirit which was eventually laid in Lane End Pond at the edge of the village.

Just north of Kirtlington village lies Northbrook Farm, although there is nothing remaining of the old manor house which once graced the location. The house was the home of Sir James Dashwood, but after his death in 1779 he was reluctant to leave the property and made the inhabitants' lives a misery by his constant ghostly presence. As you might suppose, he was banished to one of the ponds which can still be seen on the farm today. And, as we have also come to expect, it is said that when the pond dries out his spirit will return.

When Thomas Money of South Moreton described how he had been watering horses at a trough only to have a white apparition appear above the yard causing the horses to stampede in panic, no-one was terribly surprised; ever since William Field had hanged himself in his barn at back in 1804 his ghost had been troubling the rest of the village. Passers-by were terrified by the sight of him appearing in his old farm courtyard and one young boy called George Hall described how a grinning ghoul had gurned at him from behind a tree causing him considerable shock and distress. Something, it was eventually decided, had to be done.

Consequently, in the year 1850 the villagers finally appealed for help and eleven priests were summoned to perform an exorcism. Two local brothers named John and James Parkes decided to spy on the event and hid themselves under a pile of straw in the barn just before the ceremony was due to begin. As the exorcism proceeded the ghost manifested itself to the collective clergy and agreed to depart provided the group accepted his conditions for doing so. As the price for his departure, Money's ghost asked for either 'the cock on the dunghill or the two mice under the straw'. Puzzled, the priests conferred and decided that the cockerel would be most appropriate, and the spirit immediately tore the poor bird to pieces. The two 'mice' watching from their hiding place were presumably most relieved. Money's spirit was ceremonially staked to the bottom of the farm pond never to be seen again. Unless it should ever dry out I suppose.

Many of these pond stories seem rooted quite far back in the past but some do have (relatively) recent updates. Take the case of Nanny Martin. Martin was a servant who lived at Wick Farm in Headington, just behind the present crematorium, at the end of the eighteenth century. She was reputed to be a

Wick Farm, home to the unfortunate Nanny Martin

POND MEMORIES

The Roman Well, beside which Nanny's body was found

kind-hearted woman who would welcome visitors who came to the farm to take advantage of the clear spring* which was claimed to have healing properties if applied to the eyes. Sadly, one of her visitors took advantage of her good nature and she was found murdered beside the well and subsequently buried in the nearby churchyard. Despite her name she was still a relatively young woman.

Of course, as we might expect given the nature of her death, her spirit did not rest peacefully and her ghost was frequently seen near the well or walking along the lanes towards Woodperry and Stanton St John in the nineteenth century. She seems to have been especially fond of the company of one of the local men by the name of Green since he reported a girlish figure joining him on his walks past the farm on several occasions. On one memorable evening he had consumed a few too many drinks at one of the local inns and tried to kiss the

---

* Actually a Roman well covered by a well house dating back to around 1660.

flirtatious phantom but she faded hastily away when he reached out to her.

It also seems that Nanny was fond of helping local scrumpers. According to Joseph Drewett, when he was a young man he and a group of friends crept into the farm one day with the aim of purloining some apples from a particularly tasty tree in the orchard. As they drew nearer the tree began to shake and apples rained down around them. They hastily grabbed what they could and fled through the orchard gate – which promptly slammed itself shut behind them. Sometime later, one of the farm labourers who was especially fond of russet apples climbed up a tree to collect a basketful. As he reached the leafy canopy he was surprised to see the ghost of Nanny Martin sitting on a branch above him; so surprised in fact that he fell right out of the tree and fled in terror.

The farmhands were clearly well used to her appearances. A carter named Morris told how whenever he returned the horses to the farm at twilight the yard gate would mysteriously open for him, accompanied by the rustling of a silk dress. This rustling was also heard by an old man named William Girl who was walking along the path from Woodperry with a friend when they encountered what they described as a tall woman dressed in silk. The woman turned and vanished into a hedge, apparently making considerable noise in the process. The shock was so great that Girl was ill for some time afterwards. It may have been this last encounter which caused the inevitable backlash; Nanny Martin's ghost was laid in the pool which came to be known as Nanny Martin's Pond. I like to think that the location was chosen because the pond was, presumably, fed from the spring she had so loved during her life.

The pond was filled in some years later which may explain why there continued to be reports of a female figure flitting around the fields in the area and walking from the farmhouse to the orchard as late as the 1980s. There reports sparked reminiscences from people who had experienced odd activity while staying at Wick Farm itself. One correspondent remembered seeing Martin back in the 1920s and another recalled being afraid to go upstairs in the farmhouse because the door to the attic, which was always closed every night, would be found wide open every morning.

There had been reports of odd activity in the building even before this time. A previous inhabitant, Miss Ely, was dressing for a party one evening in front of her mirror and was alarmed to suddenly notice the reflection a face peering over her shoulder. Turning hastily around she discovered that she was entirely alone in her room; on turning back to the mirror she was relieved to see that the phantom face had disappeared. A later owner claimed that he had moved out of the house because of odd noises and lights in the night. He turned the management of the building to a bailiff whose wife refused to stay in the property and who revealed that when the couple had tried to paper the walls Nanny Martin (they presumed) had torn the wallpaper down. On another occasion the bailiff was visiting the property with his young granddaughter when he observed the door at one end of a room open and close, followed shortly afterwards by the door at the other end, in all the world as if an unseen presence had just crossed in front of them. He assured the child that the phenomena had been caused by the wind: she, however, was far from convinced.

In an interesting illustration of how such stories can morph and mutate, a series of letters to the *Oxford Star* newspaper told the story of *Nellie* Martin, a serving girl who threw her illegitimate baby into the well before drowning herself in a nearby pond. Not surprisingly, one writer telling this story described the well as being 'a cold and gloomy place'. The Roman Well is now a grade II listed monument so you can check out this part of the story at least for yourself; Nanny Martin may well be somewhat more reticent.

Woodperry has previous when it comes to ghosts – er – getting laid. A decade or two before the Nanny Martin killing, Woodperry House started to display some of the most common symptoms of being haunted. Ghostly moans and cries would murmur throughout the house at night and the servants reported hearing the rustling of silk passing them in the corridors, the rattling of ironwork in the fireplaces and crockery being broken by unseen hands. To the front of the house, on a large lawn, stood two summer houses and two figures, one male and one female, were sometimes glimpsed nearby at twilight. One day, when the President of Trinity College was visiting the house, he encountered a figure he did not know in the hallway; as he

Woodperry House

turned to speak to the unknown person he realised that they had vanished clean away. Presumably not being willing to be so rudely treated by a mere ghost he later returned with a group of priests and laid at least one of the ghosts in a well underneath a woodpile.

Whichever of the ghosts of Woodperry House ended up in the well should probably consider itself relatively lucky. According to a tale told to folklorist Percy Manning at around the same time by an old lady from Wheatley called Mrs East, the village had been haunted by the shade of a woman known as Betty Brown. Betty had lived around a century before and had died in, and remained to haunt, the area around Hollis Close. A full dozen Deans, Divines and diverse men of the cloth, clergymen of some sort anyway, eventually arrived and banished her spirit to Hollis Ditch. Not, perhaps, the best place to await the Day of Judgment.

And yet, we can easily trump twelve mere priests with our next haunting. Rewley House is now the primary base of Oxford University's Department for Continuing Education, but it was once a private house and home to three spinster women known locally as the 'Maidens Kendall'. After the three ladies' deaths the house fell into disrepair and acquired a reputation for being haunted, indeed the ladies could often be seen in the streets around the house, especially on the Quarter Days when the charity dole from the will of Ann Kendall was distributed – that is Lady Day, Midsummer, Michaelmas and Christmas. The 'maidens' were generally seen in the Gloucester Green and Oxpens area of the town; some reports held that appearances were solitary (Lady Ann in particular was easily recognisable by the white satin shoes she favoured while alive) but others

Rewley House, home of the Maidens Kendall, whose unsettled spirits were laid to rest under Castle Mill Bridge

asserted that they would perambulate together, in order of decreasing height, and that they came to be called the 'grey ladies'. Although they seem to have caused neither consternation nor harm, they were eventually laid to rest underneath Castle Mill Bridge by a baker's dozen of Bishops, although why it should take thirteen senior churchmen to banish such a harmless haunting is an interesting question. Perhaps they were not so harmless after all; one of the bishops involved in the ceremony was reported to have mysteriously died within the year. You will not be surprised to hear that whenever the water beneath the bridge runs low the sisters once more resume their visits to the streets of Oxford.

Notes from a Lady

JACKSON'S OXFORD JOURNAL, Oxford's local newspaper from 1753 until 1909,* is a fascinating resource and a source of endless interesting local stories, many of them relevant to the subject to hand. In the years around 1900 Jackson's featured a regular column called 'Notes from a Lady', written under the nom-de-plume Barbara Bocardo, which was to become a regular feature for over two decades. While most of her columns covered social events or other public occasions, over the Christmas period in 1900 Bocardo turned her attention to ghost stories.

One of the encounters she relates concerns a male friend who was walking along The Avenue in Kennington one summer evening when he saw a younger male acquaintance, along with a young lady whom he did not recognise, approaching him. He glanced briefly away but when his gaze returned to the young couple he realised that they were no longer in sight. Thinking nothing of it, he continued his walk and, when he encountered his friend the following day and asked what he had been doing in the area, his friend insisted that he had been elsewhere. As the writer observes, to make this a classic ghost tale the young man really should have been discovered to have died at that exact moment, or should have been encountered in that particular place at some point in the future at the very least, but alas, stories of this nature are rarely as tidy as we might prefer.

Bocardo tells a similar story about a young man who lived in North Oxford, next door to an old lady who was extremely ill

---

* After which it became the *Oxford Journal Illustrated* but remained Oxford's local paper.

and entirely housebound. Being a kindly soul, the man was in the habit of calling into the house to keep the older lady company but one day, as he gazed out of an upstairs window he was surprised and pleased to see her up and about, strolling in her garden with a member of her family. He later encountered the relative in the street and commented that he was glad that his neighbour was recovering from her illness. The relative looked puzzled and assured him that the lady was still ill and that no-one had been to visit her for some time. Again, this was no deathbed apparition; the lady lived for some months after her non-appearance.

Bocardo also offers an account of an experience of her own. Apparently she lived with her brother Richard, who seems to have been something of a stickler for punctuality, because she describes being late for breakfast one morning and hurrying her morning ablutions to make sure she was not too late arriving at the dining room. Hastily grabbing a few things, she left her bedroom and raced downstairs, but as she passed the library she glanced inside to observe Richard standing beside a bookshelf opposite the door. Relieved that she was going to be there before him she reduced her hectic pace to a leisurely saunter and entered the dining room only to 'observe in horror that there was another Richard seated at the breakfast table'. For a second she 'wondered which was the phantom and which the solid flesh, but the way in which the one before my eyes was helping himself to bacon and clamouring for coffee decided the question'. She was nonetheless considerably shaken and, being aware of how such apparitions may portend some future tragedy, feared the worst; thankfully a subsequent lack of any significant family misfortune led her to discount any significance to her sighting.*

Curiously, in a corollary she mentions that her friend from the first story later 'saw a well-known tradesman in St. Giles and on reflection remembered that he had been dead for some months', so perhaps we can take some comfort in noting that the normal narrative conventions are sometimes properly observed.

Her last story is even more interesting. Bocardo had arranged to go to a concert at Balliol College with a friend she calls only B and, at the very last minute her brother decided to

---

* In fact she need not have worried; in Irish folklore encountering such a 'fetch' in the morning presaged good fortune.

accompany them. They called at B's house to collect her and the maid invited them inside. Suspecting that stepping indoors might cause a delay, and knowing her brother's distaste for such things, Barbara opted to remain on the doorstop, feeling (probably correctly) that this would ensure that her friend made haste to join them. However, as she glanced into the hallway her heart sank; in full view were a pair of knee-length ladies' boots of a kind that would need extensive lacing to put on. It seemed as if they were destined to be held up for some time after all. Luckily B made a quick appearance, already wearing another pair of boots, and rushed to join them seeming, the writer observed, almost to pass through the boots in the hallway as she passed.

Ghost boots in the hallway

Later that evening, while at the concert, B confided to her friend that her feet were cold because her boots were wet. Bocardo felt somewhat guilty that they may have unnecessarily hurried her from the house without giving her the opportunity to switch to put on a dry pair. 'Why didn't you change them then?' she asked. 'That's simple,' B replied, 'these happen to be the only pair of boots I have.' The writer was, not surprisingly, puzzled. Had she seen a pair of *ghost boots*? She herself never came to any conclusions about this weird experience but I confess to being intrigued. Ghostly people I suspect would cause most people little problem; ghostly horses possibly more so, especially if accompanied by a carriage; ghostly guinea pigs and mosquitoes even less likely. But ghost boots? Still, why not: at least we know that they have soles ...[*]

---

[*] I'll get my coat.

Looking towards the site of the old Souldern Rectory

A Vacation Visitation

ROBERT GROVE WAS A FELLOW of St John's College[*] in 1706, a time of some political upheaval in the university (universities in fact) resulting from the Oath of Allegiance which had been demanded by William and Mary in 1688. Many university fellows had declared themselves unwilling to swear such an oath and were either ejected or quietly removed from their positions as 'non-jurors'. One such unfortunate was an old friend of Grove, the Rev. Geoffrey Shaw, who had left Cambridge in advance of the edict in 1687 and was by this time Rector of the village of Souldern.

In early August 1706 Grove was travelling from the West Country back to Cambridge during the university's long vacation, and called at Souldern for a few days to catch up with his old friend and colleague. At some point during the visit Shaw shared the story of an old friend of them both who had visited him one evening some weeks earlier, another ex-St John's Fellow called John Naylor. What made this story particularly noteworthy was the fact that Naylor had died some years previously.

According to Shaw he had been sitting alone in his study late one evening, reading and smoking as was his custom, when

> the Spectre of his old Companion Mr Naylour [...] came into the room habited in a Gown & Cassock & Exactly in the same manner as he used to appear in the College when alive. Mr Shaw remembered the figure well & was therefore much surprised, but the spectre took a chair & sitting down close by him bid him not be afraid for he came to acquaint him with something that nearly concerned him. So entering into discourse together, the Spectre told

---

[*] In Cambridge rather than Oxford, but no-one is perfect.

him that their friend Mr [Arthur] Orchard was to die very suddenly & that he himself should die soon after him & therefore he came to forewarn him that he might prepare himself accordingly.*

After delivering this somewhat devastating news it seems that the two men conversed for some time, particularly about old comrades. Shaw enquired as to whether any of their deceased friends were with Naylor on the other side but was disappointed when told that Naylor had seen none of them.

Naturally, Shaw asked questions about the nature of the afterlife, but it seems that Naylor was either unwilling or unable to supply many details – although he did reveal that he was both well and happy in his new state. The man and manifestation spoke together for around two hours but eventually Naylor returned from whence he came and Shaw spent the rest of the night pacing around his room and considering what had just happened. I bet he did.

Grove was by all accounts a sceptical man when it came to the supernatural, so he was undoubtedly surprised to hear such a tale from his friend and, quite probably, paid it little heed. (To be fair Shaw, who had been Professor of Mathematics and Geometry, had been something of a sceptic himself before his momentous encounter.) In any case Grove had to make haste back to Cambridge and so bade Shaw farewell before continuing his journey. En-route he called in on another acquaintance, yet another St John's Fellow by the name of Peter Clark, and on enquiring about college news was informed of the recent death of Arthur Orchard. At which point he probably began to take the tale a little more seriously, especially when news arrived at Cambridge later that year that Geoffrey Shaw had 'dropped down dead in the prayer desk at Soulderne while reading the second lesson of Evensong 17 Nov. 1706'.

The whole event was published in a 1707 pamphlet entitled *A Very True and Faithful Account of the Apparition or Ghost of Mr John Naylor*' and further accounts were published in *The Eagle*,** *The Gentleman's Magazine*, and various newspapers and

---

* I am really not sure this is the kindest favour you could do for an old friend, although perhaps being presented with undeniable proof of an afterlife might lessen the shock.

** The St John's College in-house magazine, not the boys' comic ...

publications since. But what was the truth in the story? Given the backgrounds of those involved pure hoaxing seems unlikely – the nature of the 'joke' would certainly have been in very poor taste and would hardly have enhanced a university career. Did Shaw simply dream the entire encounter (although, if it was a dream it seems to have been a particularly prescient one) or was this a genuine visitation from an apparitional academic? As *The Eagle* writer commented: 'What furthers my belief of its being a true vision, and not a dream, is Mr Grove's incredulity of stories of this nature. Considering them both as men of learning and integrity, the one would not first have declared, nor the other have spread the same, were not the matter itself serious and real.'

The Swindlestock Tavern

The Students are Revolting

It was a running joke in the 1980s that banks were being converted into wine bars but here is an example of that process in reverse. And it ought to serve as a warning that, should you find fault with any drink you may be served in an Oxford tavern, you should be careful how strongly you express your disapproval: two students who found themselves in this situation caused scores of deaths and soured the atmosphere in the town for 600 years ...

The Feast Day of St Scolastica (an entirely co-incidentally named Italian saint) falls on 10 February and on this day in 1355 a group of students were drinking in the Swyndlestock Tavern, a Carfax inn owned by the then Mayor of Oxford, John de Beresford.

Oxford was a very different place in the fourteenth century. The Black Death had killed over a quarter of the population and the student body, supposedly studying theology and destined for careers as clerks or in the priesthood, were engaged in what can only be described as internecine warfare with the townsfolk; assaults and stabbings were a popular local pastime. The student body resented what they saw as the inflated prices they were charged for rents, not to mention entertainment in the taverns of the city, whereas the townsfolk felt aggrieved by the behaviour of the students and the fact that the civic authorities were unable to exercise any control over them, a privilege that was reserved for the University Chancellor alone.

In this somewhat febrile atmosphere publican John Croidon (aka John of Croydon) brought drinks to a group of students who were out celebrating the Saint's Day in the Swyndlestock. Two of the students, Walter Spryngeheuse and Roger de

Chesterfield, decided that they had been served cheap, or possibly watered, wine and complained to Croiden who is reported to have responded with 'stubborn and saucy language' which, in turn, led to one of the students throwing a quart flagon of the supposedly unsatisfactory wine at his head. Unfortunately for the student group De Beresford was also in the tavern that afternoon, along with a number of friends and members of his family who all stepped in to support Croiden. The incident soon spiralled out of control and the ensuing brawl in the tavern spilled out into the street. It was at this point that everything kicked off.

Another member of the town authorities had also been drinking in the pub that afternoon, the Bailiff Robert de Lardiner, and because his authority did not extend to controlling the behaviour of the students his response was to have had the bells of the Church of St Martin's at Carfax rung out as a call to arms to the people of the town – who took this very literally by appearing en-masse with whatever makeshift weapons they could find. In a belated attempt to control the situation the mayor asked the Chancellor of the University to discipline the fighting students, but the Chancellor did exactly the opposite and responded by sounding the chimes of the University Church of St Mary's; two hundred students responded and battle was, quite literally, joined until night fell and the two sides retreated to lick their wounds.

The next morning the University Chancellor issued an edict that no-one was permitted to carry weapons within the walls of Oxford, an announcement which enraged the people of the town as he had no authority over the non-university population. As the Westgate opened at dawn a large crowd of people from the surrounding countryside surged through with a battle cry of 'Havoc! Havoc! Smyt fast, give gode knocks!' and clutching a variety of supposedly proscribed weapons, including cudgels, axes and even a number of bows. Clearly aware of the danger, bands of students armed themselves in return and attempted to close the gates, but by the afternoon over two thousand local people had forced their way into the city and set about systematically dragging students from their lodgings and beating and even killing them. Obviously, the students responded in kind. The rioting continued for two days after which thirty townspeople lay dead; the students had fared worse with sixty-three fatalities among their number.

Coincidentally the King, Edward III, was staying at Woodstock at the time and De Beresford, in his capacity as Mayor, rode out to complain about the behaviour of the university students, who, he declared, had illegally forced the city gates closed, robbed and beaten townsfolk and even set fire to part of the town. The king responded by instructing five judges to investigate the riots. Unfortunately for the Mayor and council, the enquiry decided in favour of the university and imposed severe penalties on the town. The mayor and 61 leading citizens were ordered to make a penitential appearance in the university church and additionally to make a public payment of 63 pennies (one for each student killed) to the Chancellor each year. Furthermore, almost total control of the civic functions of Oxford was passed to the university. Over the years civic control gradually returned to the city,* but the annual humiliation of the council continued until 1825, at which point the Mayor decided that enough was enough and refused point blank to participate. It could be argued that the whole episode did not finally come to a conclusion until 1955, when the university offered the Mayor an Honorary Doctorate and the city responded by making the Chancellor a freeman of Oxford.

A local saying from considerably later runs:

> *Chronica si penses, cum pungent Oxoniensis,*
> *Post aliquot menses, volat ira per Angliginenses.*

Which (very) loosely translates as:

> *Mark the chronicles aright,*
> *When Oxford scholars fall to fight.*
> *Before many months are expired,*
> *England will with war be fired.*

Perhaps the author is suggesting that the Hundred Years War, during which the riot took place, might have been rather shorter had Oxford academics been less quarrelsome.

For a while the building which used to be the Swyndlestock Tavern was known as Marygold House (it is now Abbey

---

* Oxford eventually became a city in 1542.

House) and was a bakery until around a century ago when, in a wonderful piece of linguistic irony, it became occupied by a bank. An inscription carved into the stone of the building commemorates its role in a pivotal piece of Oxford history.

Well, that is a lot of, admittedly interesting, history for a thin return. I have no reports of any kind of odd phenomena from staff currently working in Abbey House but Graham, who worked in the bank in the 1960s, distinctly remembered an uncomfortable atmosphere when working in one part of the building, something that gave rise to rumours among the rest of the staff about a ghostly presence although there were, as far as he was aware, no sightings of anything unusual. 'It was just a chill feeling, as if someone was always looking over your shoulder. I didn't ever see anything that might have been a ghost, but we all thought that there might have been one.'

I have also been told that the screams of the dead still ring out from the site of the start of the riots in the early hours of the morning, but I have not been able to track down anyone who has heard this in recent years, and I suspect that the story originated as a scary addendum to a local ghost tour. Or perhaps, given the improvements in town–gown relationships, the St Scholastica Day riot has finally been forgotten on the far side of the Great Divide.

Unearthly De-lights

THE VALE OF WHITE HORSE IS, of course, best known for the Uffington White Horse, the oldest hill carving in the country and still looking good at 3,500 years old, but the Vale also offers a slightly less well-known source of weirdness: unexplained lights in the sky. One report from a family driving past the Horse towards Swindon back in 1981 described how they watched a triangular formation of lights drift across the Downs above their heads. Stopping the car and climbing outside for a better look they were amazed to see that, rather than being individual lights, the formation marked the corners of a gigantic triangular vehicle passing overhead. 'It was solid (it blacked out the stars) and noiseless and very big. I have been to air shows, and once saw a Vulcan bomber fly close overhead [and] I would scale it up to 3 or 4 times larger at the very least,' commented one of the family. Very much unlike a Vulcan, the unknown craft passed overhead entirely silently.

A driver travelling in the opposite direction on the same road one evening in November 2005 saw an unusual white bright light behind him travelling, as he described it, eastward, like himself. In this case the light seemed to parallel the car and the intensity of the brightness rose and fell, as did the apparent size of the apparition, varying from seeming to be as large as the full moon down to a single star-like point. The encounter reportedly lasted between 5 and 10 minutes and seemed to be accompanied by an odd buzzing sound which, according to the witness, seemed to be disturbing local animals.*

---

* At the risk of sounding overly sceptical so early on in this section, the planet Venus was an incredibly bright object in the south-western sky at

View across the Vale

Across the county the *Oxford Mail* has published a variety of witness reports of anomalous aerial activity. For example, an unknown object was observed moving over Witney in 2007. 'It appeared as a slow-moving, orange light – as if a light aircraft was in flames. It was moving in a northerly direction, then bore round to the east. It disappeared in the direction of Woodstock. There was no sound at all. It was very strange.'

Similarly, in Abingdon in 2008 a 'red and black grenade shaped object' was seen flying silently over rooftops along Abingdon High Street. 'This thing was not a light aircraft but definitely 3D grenade shape. The object seemed to be suspended in mid-air without any means of support; it was not floating or gliding ... [it] was under power and flying in a constant straight line, flying through sky like an upright egg, not horizontal like a cigar. The object disappeared over the High St and was no

---

that time and would have been ideally placed to generate a report like this. I'm not sure I have any reports of planets buzzing though. Lest you find this suggestion unlikely, I will just point out that in 2013 the Indian Army spent *months* surveying alleged 'Chinese surveillance drones', which eventually turned out to be misreported sightings of Venus.

longer in the sky where it should have been; there was no cloud cover; it was no larger than two new mini cars side by side.'

There were other UFO* sightings from the town, one in 1989 of a parachute-shaped object which moved entirely unlike a parachute (there is even a YouTube video of the sighting) and another from 2016 from near the airfield.**

In any case, while Abingdon may be something of a minor hotspot, other parts of the county seem unwilling to be left out.

A report, released by the government as part of its Freedom of Information obligations no less, included an incident near Broughton in November 2000 in which a group of children who were playing outside were surrounded by a strange circle of moving blue lights which descended around them. Not unsurprisingly they fled the scene.

How about this from Blackbird Leys in 2010? The witness and two friends were standing outside one evening when 'all of a sudden a bright light appeared travelling across the sky at speed. I grabbed the phone and took a photo as the lights were travelling across the sky and disappeared as they headed towards Cowley. Then another red light appeared ... it seemed like a roundish shape with a trail of smoke round it. They were definitely not an aircraft or Chinese lanterns. But don't know what they were.'

A witness described a sighting in Banbury in July 2018:

> I was amazed at what I was looking at. This object was very big given the altitude and distance it appeared to be and was cigar shaped and with a light that seemed to move along its lateral axis. I got my phone camera on it and watched it for a good 5 minutes, flashing lights and rotating on its own central axis which had the appearance of it changing its shape. I quickly ascertained that this was no balloon as it remained pretty much stationary while the clouds were moving to the south. After filming for a few minutes I thought I may have time to get my tripod. At that point, the craft

---

* These days UFOs are more usually called UAPs (Unidentified Aerial Phenomena).
** A fact which might well mitigate the 'unidentified' part of the tag. Incidentally, I have an undated report of another strangely silent object displaying flashing lights seen above Yarnton. Travelling in the direction of Kidlington Airport. Which has a gliding school ... Sometimes reaching for Occam's razor is the only solution.

Ploughley Road – an odd spot for a UFO encounter

accelerated upwards until it was out of sight and very unfortunately not on film. The best bits I never got to record.

Another observer of the same event described the object as a large black cylinder hovering in the sky. Interestingly, another 8-minute encounter with a slowly climbing unidentified object was reported from the same area in 2006.

Here is another report of something above Blackbird Leys from May 2011, when three witnesses saw a cylindrical shape at around 10.30 one evening. One commented 'I was standing out in my back garden when some triangular lights flew into view and hovered approximately 400 to 500 ft above the house, moving slowly with a humming sound. Then the formation changed shape to a long cylinder, with one green light at the front and two red lights at the back ... before flying slowly away to the south of Oxford.' No-one reported such an object arriving in the city.

Oxfordshire can even boast a Close Encounter of the Third Kind* from October 1974, when two 13-year-old boys from Bicester walking along Ploughley Road just outside the town were frightened by an odd green light glowing in the sky. As if this was not enough, they noticed shortly afterwards that they were being followed by a figure which they described as large

---

* An encounter of the first kind (CE1K) is a simple light in the sky sighting; a CE2K is a sighting with some form of physical effects such as burnt vegetation; a CE3K is a meeting with aliens (hence the film title). The scheme was devised by J. Allen Hynek has been unofficially extended as far as CE7K which involves the creation of human-alien hybrids. By this point the scheme may have lost its scientific rigour.

and hunched over and which they assumed was associated with the green object. They rushed home as fast as they could and were later reported as being in a state of 'fear and shock'. The source of the lights and the identity of the mysterious figure were never determined.

Here is a slightly more detailed recollection to round this section off. Ted and Ian were sitting in the kitchen of Ted's house in Thame one night in April 2018, having a generally convivial evening with a few beers, when Ted glanced out of the window to see something very odd in the skies above the town.

'I happened to look outside very late in the evening,' Ted commented, 'only to see what looked like two giant blue lights moving across the sky. I couldn't believe what I was seeing and asked Ian if he could see it too.' The two men rushed outside to get a better look and watched what they described as 'a patch of glowing blue light travelling at speed across the sky, illuminating the clouds.' 'We were fascinated and not a little scared,' added Ian. 'The lights weren't moving like a plane and there was no noise like an aircraft or helicopter would have made; it was all eerily smooth and silent. We had had a couple of beers but were in no way drunk. In any case, we both saw the same thing.'

The men could come to no conclusion as to the source of the strange phenomenon and after watching it disappear behind some nearby buildings they retired back to the warmth of the house to pour a final soothing drink.

These same lights were actually seen across a wide swathe of countryside along a corridor between Banbury and High Wycombe. Witness descriptions varied widely; some reported an eerie blue glow with others describing two enormous blue circles, like giant spectral eyes, moving across the sky. One camper in Chinnor described the light as 'a flashing purple orb behind dense cloud cover. It was just moving slowly and pulsating; flashing'. Many reports described a beam descending from a body hidden by low cloud while others said that the beam began at the ground and shot upwards to illuminate the cloud cover. Possible explanations offered included transport aircraft flying to or from one of the local airfields, lights from a ground-based party or a local laser show. Being a mid-week evening the latter two options were unlikely and the lights

THE OX-FILES

An eye in the sky?

were deemed far too bright to be the result of any aircraft activity. Luckily local social media quickly stepped in to fill the information void and the actinic activity was soon recast as an alien scouting mission from parts, or planets, unknown.

Sadly, for those who attempted to seek for a supernatural source or assign an alien attribution to these lights anyway, it was quickly noted that this corridor closely matched the route of a major railway line, and the source of the blue lights was explained away as a Structure Gauging Train, a specialist vehicle equipped with a blue laser which can be used to accurately measure the integrity of railway tracks or overhead power cables. So, case solved: a drearily mundane explanation after all. All well and good – if you believe it of course. Sober or not, Ted and Ian were still tempted to contact the Campaign for Real Aliens …

Haunted People

Jessie Gibbs was known as something of a character in Wantage. She ran a grocery shop in what is now the Post Office Vaults but her main claim to fame was a certain tendency for tidiness and a fondness for routine.

Jessie lived in Trinder Road in the town and her evening schedule ran like a well-oiled machine: check the house was tidy then retire upstairs to bed. Jessie lived alone so it came as something of a surprise when she came downstairs one morning to find one of her kitchen drawers slightly open. Shrugging to herself she closed the drawer and continued with her day. She took extra care that evening to check that everything was organised, so was somewhat perturbed to come down the following morning to discover that the same drawer was fully open and some of the contents had been spilled onto the floor.

To her increasing dismay this pattern of events continued to escalate. Each morning Jessie would come downstairs to an ever-increasing scene of confusion; irrespective of how carefully she had checked her home the previous night the morning always delivered a far from pleasant surprise. Worse still whatever was causing all this disruption became increasingly destructive, on one occasion locking a bathroom door from inside the room and smashing a mirror on the wall.

Eventually the stress began to take its toll and she decided that the only way to recover her previous sedate and settled existence was to move and leave her troublesome tormentor to bother the new owners. Consequently, she put her house onto the market, bought another property in Mill Street (into which she also transferred her business) and prepared to leave all her troubles behind.

Let's take a brief break from Jessie's problems and discuss a tale from nineteenth-century Lancashire. According to T. Keightley writing in *The Fairy Mythology*, farmer George Gilbertson found his household haunted by a boggart, a malevolent spirit which terrorised his household, teasing the cows, tormenting the children and curdling the milk. Tiring of the constant disruption the family decided that they had no choice but to flee from their persecutor and so piled up their belongings onto a cart and prepared to depart their home forever. As they were tying the final ropes about the cart a family friend wandered over to say goodbye. 'Well, Georgey,' said he, 'and soa you're leaving t'ould hoose at last?' Before Gilbertson could answer a voice from within a milk churn called out 'Aye, aye, we're flitting, ye see'. Realising that they would be taking their troubles with them wherever they went the family unpacked their belongings and were forced to endure their lot until 'the boggart tired of the game'.

How is this diversion relevant? Well, Jessie Gibbs unpacked her belongings in her new home, checked that everything was tidy downstairs as was her wont, and retired to bed. When she came downstairs the following morning she found a kitchen drawer was open. Some days later a tap in the kitchen mysteriously turned itself on and a lamp dimmed during a meeting with friends, accompanied by a strange chill descending on the room …

Fortunately, after some months had passed the disruptive events in Jessie's home gradually began to decrease and eventually ceased completely leaving Jessie free, at last, to resume her measured and organised life.*

Let's compare and contrast here. Blacksmith Thomas Hall and his wife Ann lived in Little Tew in the nineteenth century and at some point also seem to have attracted the interest of an entity of a paranormal or supernatural nature. Although nothing was ever seen in their home, they would often have their meals disturbed by the sound of an invisible cockerel

---

* There is another telling of this story in which Jessie moves house, expressing the hope that her (less troublesome) ghost follows her. I far prefer the version here, which was related by a Gibbs family friend, but it does highlight the difficulty in getting to the truth behind *any* ghost story …

The old blacksmith's, Little Tew

crowing loudly at the table and the rattling and crashing of crockery in closed cupboards. Despite the unmistakable sounds of damage occurring nothing was ever actually found to have been broken.

Finding living with these phenomena to be unpalatable to say the least, the family packed up and moved to Hook Norton where Thomas Hall set up another smithy business. Unfortunately for them, much like Jessie Gibbs, the noises followed them to their new home. When Mrs Hall's mother, who lived with the couple at the time, went to bed one night she was frightened to hear the sound of groaning coming from beneath her pillow. She seized a knife and drove it through the pillow and into the bed and then watched with horrified fascination as blood oozed from the tear. Nervously she lifted the pillow: there was nothing underneath.

In another attempt to escape their unseen persecutor the Halls moved once again, this time to Enstone where Mr Hall stoically set about re-establishing his business – although this time the phenomena became more physical. While they were in Enstone they made the acquaintance of a local man called Samuel Jeffries who later told the story of their misfortunes. Jeffries reported that when he visited Hall in his forge an unseen hand would seem to wrestle for control of the hammer and cause Hall to mistime his strokes. On one occasion, as he sat in the Halls' new home chatting with the couple, the fire-irons from the fireplace suddenly started moving and walked themselves across the room: Jeffries freely admitted that he was terrified and fled the house. Clearly the haunting had grown to a fully-fledged poltergeist infestation. Not only did the crashing from the cupboards resume but when Jeffries joined the Halls for

The old Forge, Enstone

lunch one day a voice rang out telling Ann Hall to lay another place setting. Mrs Hall hastened to comply; there would be no peace if she did not, she told him. Even more frighteningly, on one occasion a sound like a gunshot was heard and a bullet fell onto the kitchen table. No hole could be found in the door or any of the walls, so from whence it had appeared was a mystery none of those present could fathom.

Unfortunately, there is no tidy end to this tale. Presumably the phenomena eventually faded away, but Jefferies is silent on the matter. When he told the story in 1894 the Halls had been dead for some years and he commented that Enstone was once again free of ghosts, but he does not say whether the phenomena had already ceased or, quite literally, died with them.

I have an, admittedly rather pale, modern equivalent to these tales from a girl named Sally who spent some time working at a number of jobs around the county. Her story started while she was working at a shop in Didcot and began to sense a presence in the corner of the counter area whenever she was alone. Slightly unnerved, but not actually frightened, she found herself constantly glancing towards the corner as if expecting something to manifest itself at any time. For many weeks nothing did, and Sally began to wonder whether she was suffering from stress, anxiety or some other condition which might make her jumpy. She need not have worried about her mental health because after about a month of experiencing this presence she was finally granted a glimpse of her phantom observer; or rather not, since all she could actually see was a strange misty shape floating in the very corner which had held her attention for so long.

'It was less like mist than the reflection of a figure, but as if seen in glass rather than a mirror' was how she described the apparition. 'Almost as soon as I had spotted it, it disappeared again'. Sally was unsure whether to be disturbed by the sighting or whether to be relieved that she had not been imagining the entire experience. Over the next few weeks the figure made increasingly frequent reappearances, but never became any more clearly visible. Curiously, although Sally told other members of staff of her experiences none of the other members of the team ever saw anything in the corner of the shop, even when she squealed and pointed when the figure appeared. After a while Sally decided that the ghostly appearances and the almost perpetual sense of apprehension that the phenomenon engendered were making her life too stressful and so she left the shop and took up a similar position elsewhere in the town.

For a while Sally enjoyed her new job but after a couple of months she started to feel oddly nervous again and, some weeks later, she was working alone when she spotted a vaguely familiar misty shape hovering in the stockroom. As before, the figure made increasingly frequent appearances over the next few weeks, but Sally felt less threatened this time and continued to work at the shop.

Sadly, Sally split with her long-term boyfriend at around this time and perhaps it was this change in her personal circumstances which meant that she started to become anxious once more. In any case Sally decided that the area held few attractions for her and moved back to Woodstock with her parents. Needing to find work quickly she began working in a nearby restaurant. 'It was nothing like working in the shops,' she said, 'it was a completely fresh start. I was even on the management team!'

Sally happily settled into her new position without any problems until one day she glanced up from serving a customer and noticed a misty shape forming in the corner of the bar area ... Sally no longer works in a shop or bar and is, much to her relief, entirely free of any further apparitional attention.

I am uncertain what to make of this story. Were these apparitions some kind of external manifestation of her own inner anxieties? This is certainly a possibility since no-one else was ever aware of the shapes that she kept reporting. None of the places where she worked had any particular history of hauntings and it would be an amazing co-incidence if all of the three places where she worked should have experienced random, identical, ghostly manifestations.

So, a collection of oddly personal encounters and if I were to suggest any kind of conclusion arising from this section I suppose it would have to be this: sometimes it is places that are haunted – and sometimes it's *people* ...

A Parson Investigates

THIS STORY MIGHT ALSO have featured in our section on witches, but since it developed into something very much more than an encounter with a fortune-telling visitor I think that it deserves to stand alone. The tale was first described by the Rev. Edgar Hewlett and published in an 1854 pamphlet titled *'Personal Recollections of the Little Tew Ghost"* and relates to the years 1838/9 when he was an Oxfordshire parson.

As part of his usual pastoral duties Hewlett would often call into Little Tew and became well acquainted with a number of the villagers, including a young woman named Hannah. Hannah answered a knock at her door one day to find an old woman offering to tell her fortune, doubtless in exchange for the usual monetary recompense. Being a staunchly pious girl, she told the woman in no uncertain terms that she would have no truck with fake fortune tellers and that she should leave immediately. The old woman retorted that despite Hannah's disbelief she would nonetheless tell her a true fortune, namely that she would be married within three months. She even described her future husband. Hannah became very upset and slammed the door in her face only to glance down to see, in a very odd detail to the story, a newt clinging to her dress. For some reason this caused her to become very distressed and

---

* More fully: *Personal Recollections of the Little Tew Ghost, Reviewed in Connection with the Lancashire Bogle, and the Table-Talking and Spirit-Rapping of the Present Day. By Edgar Hewlett, Minister of the Gospel, Wigan, Lancashire.* This pamphlet also features the aside in the earlier Jessie Gibbs story.

The village of Little Tew

she immediately fell to the ground suffering from some sort of seizure.

After this encounter her health was badly affected; she began to experience regular bouts of convulsions which eventually became so bad that she was forced to give up her work as a servant and go to stay with relatives to recover. Luckily, with the passage of time Hannah made a good recovery and, within the three months predicted by her mysterious visitor, did in fact become married to a local man – one in fact, who closely matched the description she had been given.

Everyone presumed that the story was over at this point; a happy ever after conclusion if ever there was one. Sadly, when Rev. Hewlett next met Hannah she was in something of an unfortunate state; in the intervening period she had been blessed with an infant child, but correspondingly cursed by a haunting. From all parts of her house unearthly noises could be heard 'being sometimes like a scratching noise, at other times as a moaning sound, and frequently as a shrill whistle.' Obviously, she was terrified by these noises and had, once again, started to experience extreme fits of shaking. These sounds tormented Hannah for a number of weeks and then, as was the case with the Hall family, whatever was tormenting her began to become physically active.* The bottles of medicinal tonic which a local doctor had supplied to help with Hannah's condition were regularly hurled down from the shelf where they were stored and sometimes when she had poured a dose to drink the vessel would be forcibly dashed from her hand, often so fiercely that it would break upon the flagstone floor. In the end a neighbour had to take custody of the bottles and the poor girl was forced to go next door to take her medication.

Unfortunately, while this solution at least allowed Hannah to take her medicine it did little to alleviate the mischief which continued to spread around the family home. As Hannah sat beside the fire unseen hands would tug at her skirts or tear her apron completely away and deposit it in another part of the house. Thumping sounds would come from the upper floors, a kneading trough lid rattled and crashed of its own accord and on one occasion one of the bedroom windows was smashed by an unseen, and never found, projectile.

These weird and disturbing events became the subject of much local gossip and speculation, but once voices started to ring out in the house opinion was divided as to whether or not Hannah was somehow faking the phenomena: why she might wish to do so no-one could say. One strongly opinionated neighbour, a doughty woman who ran an alehouse in the village, breezed into the house and went upstairs declaring her intention to examine the broken bedroom window. As she entered the room an unseen force lifted her clean off her feet and into the air where she remained for a second before being gently set back down on her feet again. In a state of some terror she fled the cottage and took to her bed for three days. Since she thereafter refused to set foot in the building again, I think we can assume that she had become convinced that the haunting was genuine.

This intrusion seems to have encouraged the boggart, poltergeist or whatever was plaguing the house because its

---

* Two similar hauntings in one small village: what can have made Little Tew so psychically special?

vocalisations became both more comprehensible and, sadly, more reprehensible; it began speaking clearly and 'using very vulgar language – and sometimes swearing dreadfully'. A group of sympathetic neighbours came around to hold a prayer service in an attempt to calm the situation, only for a ghostly voice to join in with a loud 'amen'. One of the participants summoned up the courage to ask the intrusive spirit who it was and why it was there. The only answer he received was a fiendish and dismissive laugh. A later interrogator did manage to hold a question-and-answer session during which the voice claimed to be a ghost and gave details of its name and life history: all of which proved, on investigation, to be entirely false.

By now the story had reached the local press and hundreds of curious spectators had passed through the village. There was even a rumour that the Rector and Fellows of Exeter College (Exeter held the title to the village) were going to come and banish the unruly spirit, but sadly the academics kept a safe distance. The prayer meetings continued (it seems they offered some solace to the family, if no relief from the haunting) and sometimes an odd shrill voice could be heard joining in with the hymns. Sometimes the voice even requested a particular hymn and would join in enthusiastically – odd behaviour for such a mischievous and troublesome presence.

Hannah's health continued to suffer; sometimes she found the infestation so vexatious that she would go into spasms leaving her unable to unclench her jaw for many hours at a time. The poltergeist became increasingly aggressive, throwing objects at her head including a saucepan, a stool and even a hatchet. Thankfully she was never seriously hurt. More worryingly, on one occasion her baby was snatched from her arms and thrown towards the fire; luckily the child was rescued unharmed.

The boggart (or whatever the presence was) also started stealing objects and hiding them away. One day Hannah's wedding ring vanished and as she was lamenting her loss to a friend a voice from nowhere announced that they would find it wrapped up in the handkerchief which lay upon the table. Sure enough, the ring turned out to be exactly where the voice had promised. Because of Hannah's declining health her mother had come to stay with the family and while she was there the key to the front door went missing and could not be found anywhere. 'Depend on it, that thing has got it hid somewhere,' commented the mother, only for a shrill voice to reply, 'It's in the pail of water, it's in the pail of water!' A bucket of water was indeed standing nearby and the old woman put her hand into it to feel for the key. Unable to find it she exclaimed, 'Drat that lying thing; it is not here,' whereupon the same shrill voice quickly reiterated 'It's in the pail of water!' Once again the old woman put her hand into the water, making a more thorough examination this time, and there indeed was the key standing on its end against the side. After her discovery a stifled and mocking laugh rang through the cottage.

Eventually Hannah's mother departed and her sister came to take her place. This young woman had brought with her a (strictly medicinal) bottle of porter which she kept upstairs in a chest in her bedroom but one day the sisters were in the courtyard peeling potatoes when they heard a crash from the kitchen and rushed inside to find the bottle had somehow been transported downstairs and smashed on the floor.

One evening two local men, both somewhat the worse for drink, came by the cottage and began to crash around shouting for the ghost to show itself, while banging sticks against the furniture and swearing copiously. They were summarily ejected from the property but the damage had been done; as if the voice hadn't been offensive enough before, from this point it swore and blasphemed constantly, something which clearly upset the devout family.

By this time, as Hewlett comments

> ... being so continually harrassed, the poor man and his wife could get but little rest, nor did they like to be left alone in the house; for in the dead of the night this intruder would perch himself near the bed, and sometimes on the pillow, and crow or chirp in a frightful manner; and on more than one occasion has lifted them from the bed, and laid them down again without altering their position, and apparently with as much care as a tender nurse would use towards a sleeping babe.

Not a comfortable situation.

Two men who lived nearby did offer to stay the night in support of the couple, but they too found themselves lifted bodily upwards out of their beds. This time the poltergeist was not as gentle as before and dropped them down rather roughly.

One of the men was awoken by something hitting the bed and he reached out to grab it only to recoil on finding himself clutching something cold and slippery. On examination it turned out that a collection of rushlights[*] had been lifted from a shelf and hurled in his direction.

Theories as to the cause of all these mysterious phenomena abounded. The villagers generally believed that the old woman who had visited Hannah long before had cast a bewitchment upon her; the gentlemen farmers of the locality preferred to believe that Hannah was somehow faking the whole thing and went so far as to call in a skilled ventriloquist to attempt to replicate the voices, something he singularly failed to do.

Other investigators also took their turn. Rev. Hewlett, a local doctor and a friend he identifies as Mr. K. all examined the house closely but found nothing suspicious; the doctor even peered into the young woman's throat looking for vocal abnormalities with no greater result. One man who asked to examine the property picked up and inspected a stool only to have it thrown against the back of his legs as he left. The ghost's behaviour did not improve and it even took to following Hannah to chapel, tugging at her clothes and snatching her hymn book from her hands.

One Monday a young girl from the village came to Hewlett, who was staying with his friend Mr K. in the village at the time, saying that Hannah was in a particularly bad way because the ghost had been swearing loudly and had just thrown a saucepan at her. This seems to have been the last straw for the Reverend and he hurried across to her cottage. He found her with two visitors who had come all the way from Banbury to witness the haunting and, indeed, a whispering and murmuring could be heard coming from within the walls. As poor Hannah and the various visiting parties discussed the sounds a sepulchral voice suddenly boomed out shouting 'You're a fool, you're a fool'. Hewlett knew what had to be done:

> The unearthly voice was exactly in front of me, as though I had stood face to face with the adversary. I could have placed my finger on the very spot from whence the voice issued, it was so awfully

---

[*] The central stem of rushes soaked in fat or grease and used as a cheap alternative to candles.

distinct; I felt as though I was in the immediate presence of Satan. I stood fearlessly in the Lord's strength, and realizing in my heart those blessed portions of God's word: 'In the fear of the Lord is strong confidence ... The name of the Lord is as a strong tower [...] Resist the devil, and he shall flee from you.' With my eyes rivetted to the spot from whence the voice came, I exclaimed aloud, with boldness, 'Who are you? I defy you in the name of the Lord Jesus Christ, and in the name of Jesus I bid you depart and trouble this woman no more.'

As soon as he had finished speaking a sense of peace and stillness unexpectedly descended on the household. One of the young men said, 'I think that you have spoken properly to it, Sir,' and Hannah added, 'I do think that he is driven away'. The Reverend then blessed the cottage, everyone said prayers and amazingly Hannah announced that she was confident enough that her troubles were over that she was happy for the family to be left alone in the house. And indeed it proved so. Hannah's health quickly recovered and the family returned to the normal life they had so long been denied.

So, a happy ending, eventually, but an intriguing tale along the way. Was the family plagued by a poltergeist, bothered by a boggart, or was Hannah herself somehow responsible for this paranormal persecution? Did the Rev. Hewlett's intervention drive away the haunting spirit or was this a purely psychological cure? Of course we will never know, but personally I suspect that the boggart which had played with the family had, in the end, finally tired of the game.

The Bay Tree Cafe in Wantage, formerly the White Hart Inn

A Triad of Tragedies[*]

THE BAY TREE CAFÉ at the corner of Newbury St and Post Office Lane in Wantage has been through a number of different incarnations over the years. In a previous life the building housed the local institution that was Cleggs the Chemist and before that it was, as the address might suggest, the town Post Office. There is still an old posting slot in the wall just around the corner. Prior to this however the building housed a small tavern which traded under the name The White Hart Inn.

The 1830 Pigot's Trade Directory lists one Richard Pullen as landlord of the White Hart, a successful landlord of a relatively small inn which he ran with his wife Ann, their two young children and an older son from a previous marriage. Sadly, this happy situation was not to last, and Richard died leaving Ann to manage the business as best she could. Clearly she managed very well, because the business was thriving a few years later in 1833 when events at the pub shocked the town, the county and, indeed, the whole country.

It was an autumn evening and Ann was cleaning a deserted pub before closing when an itinerant agricultural labourer from Cumnor named George King wandered into the bar and demanded a drink and a bed for the night. Local legend adds that he cheekily asked to share Ann's bed upon which she threatened to fight him off with an iron poker should he try. Whether this exchange was the catalyst for what followed is unknown, but events soon spiralled into tragedy.

There are two versions of the tale which describe what

---
[*] Even I wouldn't sink to using Triagedies as a title ...

happened next. Both agree that she offered King a rasher of bacon which he cooked over a fire before stepping into the yard to relieve himself. After this point the two stories diverge slightly: in one version Ann is slow to serve King his ale and in a fit of temper he throws his money to the ground and, as she bends down to pick it up, he swings at her neck with his razor-sharp bean hook, decapitating her with a single blow. Offering a contrary view, the coroner at her autopsy (held round the corner at The Bear Hotel) opined that King had simply come up to the woman from behind and struck her from there. Whatever the actual circumstances of the attack, Ann's body fell to the ground and her head rolled across the floor to come to rest some distance away. Unsurprisingly, the room was instantly drenched in blood, as was George King.

With a certain degree of grisly aplomb, King reached down to Ann's body, neatly removed her purse and then hastily left the building. He did not go far, just across the road in fact to the Blue Boar, a coaching inn and therefore a rather more upmarket establishment than the White Hart, where he attempted to negotiate a room for the night, presumably partly using the money he had stolen from the murdered woman. Unfortunately for him the Blue Boar was fully booked. 'Why not try the White Hart?' suggested the landlord, a recommendation which King was, understandably, not keen to follow.

In the end he fell to talking with a local man by the name of Charles Merritt[*] and they eventually left to sleep in a loft in the marketplace near (ironically) the Bear Hotel. The following morning, assuming that he was unlikely to be implicated in the events of the previous night, King rose early and returned to work cutting beans at nearby Letcombe. Unfortunately, not everyone in Wantage had such a relaxed start to their day.

The worst morning of all was presumably had by Ann Pullen's 12-year-old stepson who also rose early that morning to go fishing. There are stories of unearthly, terrifying screams which sometimes ring out in the area of Post Office Lane, and we can only suppose that these are the echoes of the screams of the young boy as he came downstairs to discover a bar coated

---

[*] In some versions of the story this character becomes a Frenchman called Charles Meriot.

The Blue Boar and the window of room 6, which looks out towards the White Hart

in dried blood and the mutilated body of his stepmother lying amidst the carnage. In any case the authorities were soon on the case and investigations began immediately. After potential witnesses had been identified and interrogated, George King soon emerged as a prime suspect. Some of the drinkers at the Blue Boar remembered how he had refused to try to obtain lodgings at the White Hart and had further noticed that, despite the warmth of the previous evening, he had kept his coat clasped close to his chest, presumably to hide the bloodstains on his clothing.

A constable was dispatched and King was apprehended at Letcombe and arrested. Apart from his blood-splattered clothes the one critical piece of evidence against him was the discovery of an oddly bent sixpenny piece among the other coins in his possession. It was well known locally that Anne Pullen had kept a lucky bent sixpence, suspiciously like the one in King's pocket.

Under questioning King declared that while he *had* indeed been at the scene of the murder the actual culprit had been a man named Edward 'Ned' Grant. King's story was that Grant had murdered Anne Pullen and then thrust her purse into his hand telling him to clear out and never tell anyone what had happened, lest Grant should seek him out and extract a dire vengeance. Of course this story failed to impress the police, especially when no-one could remember seeing this mysterious stranger the previous day, nor had any of the locals ever even heard of such a person.

At this point King admitted to the police that he had made up the character of Ned Grant in order to try to protect the identity of the real killer: Charles Merritt. Merritt was doubtless appalled at the duplicity of his erstwhile roommate but fortunately he had a cast-iron alibi; the other drinkers in the Blue Boar agreed that he had been on the premises all night and could not possibly have been complicit in the murder across the road. The lack of blood on his clothing was probably a strong indication of his innocence too.

Eventually, despite his attempts to shift the blame away from himself, King was formally charged and taken off to Reading to stand trial. Halfway to Reading he and the accompanying constable stopped for refreshment at the Black Bull in Streatley and, as they entered the building, found themselves facing a painting of a woman bearing a striking resemblance to the murdered Anne. Again, there are two versions of the story of what happened next. In the more dramatic version King falls to his knees and cries out that the woman has followed him to Streatley and he will have to kill her all over again to be rid of her. In the more prosaic version of the tale, he simply turns to the constable and states that she didn't look so calm after he had killed her. In either case this was taken as a confession and his trial was pretty much a formality; he was sentenced to be hanged for murder.

Three days after his trial, 3 March 1834, the day of his nineteenth birthday, King went to the gallows. Now, although by the twentieth century hanging had become something of a science, in the 1830s a quick death could not be guaranteed. Those with friends or family would beg them to tug on their legs in an attempt to break their necks and thus ensure a quick death; those with money might pay someone to perform this unpleasant, if merciful, duty. The alternative was to struggle and writhe at the end of the hangman's rope: a practice ghoulishly known as 'morrissing' after the way the victims' legs would kick out as if dancing. George King had no friends or family to hand and, despite the theft of Anne's money, King had nothing with which to pay a stranger so we can probably assume that he danced his macabre morris until death claimed him. After the custom of the time, he was left at the end of the rope for an hour to ensure he was dead before being cut down.

Let us return briefly to Wantage and the Blue Boar Inn. There have long been stories of a mysterious grey lady who is said to haunt the pub. Customers have reported seeing this enigmatic figure appearing from the rear part of the building, passing through the bar area and moving upstairs. Blue Boar staff tell tales of a ghost which was regularly reported by residents of room 6 although, after a major renovation some years ago and a complete turnover of staff, no-one was entirely sure where the legendary room 6 was actually located.[*] There is nothing to link this mysterious woman with the murder at the White Hart but it is tempting to wonder whether restless spirit of Ann Pullen followed her assailant across to the Boar after her death and, unaware of his departure and subsequent execution, has continued to search fruitlessly for him ever since.[**]

Incidentally, this is very much an on-going, if sporadic, haunting. During one of my summer ghost walks in the town I stopped outside the pub to tell this story. Halfway through my narration one of the staff came out through the old carriage doorway of the building and listened for a moment. 'You're telling them about the ghost, aren't you?' she asked. 'You ought to know it's started causing trouble again'.

There are a couple of interesting corollaries to this tragic tale. After Ann's death her family laid her body in an open coffin within the White Hart, with the head suitably distant from the body to demonstrate the horrific nature of her death. Clearly unwilling to forego a commercial opportunity, the body was made available to the ghoulish stream of casual viewers who came into the pub and paid a penny for a pint of beer.

---

[*] Coincidentally, a friend called Kevin actually stayed in the Boar during the 1980s and was able to identify the room as one of the first floor bedrooms looking across the road *towards the old White Hart*.

[**] No-one has ever mentioned the spirit as missing a head however so perhaps I'm just sticking my neck out with this theory.

George King's body was cut down from the scaffold and a death mask was made of his face – presumably this would have been of interest to phrenologists and the like who would have tried to associate the physical characteristics of his face and the lumps on his head with his violent character. Everyone was in for a shock however as, on shaving his head to facilitate the mask-making, it was discovered that he had a two-inch wound beneath the hairline just above his temple. Apparently, he had sustained this injury some years earlier after a beam had struck him on the head. Its location may indicate some underlying brain damage, which might in turn offer a partial explanation of his violent and unrestrained actions in murdering Ann Pullen.

All this raises an interesting moral question: which of the parties in this sorry murder is more deserving of our disgust? Is it George King, the killer who may, or may not, have been fully in control of his emotions due to damage to part of his brain, or the family of a tragically murdered mother who were willing to put her mutilated body on public display, just so that they could sell more beer?

Clearly the incumbent of Shipton Court at Shipton-under-Wychwood, a notorious drunkard called Sir John Chandos Reade, would have been at the front of the queue for some of that sweet, sweet White Hart ale. Reade's drinking exploits were notorious; in one infamous episode after assuming the office of High Sheriff of Oxfordshire he outraged his peers by drunkenly dancing on the table at his first ever official function.

He was a heavy drinker at home as well, often becoming violent and aggressive when deep in his cups. On Sunday 28 May 1843 he rang the bell to instruct his butler, a man named Thomas Sinden, to bring him another bottle to the first-floor dining room. What happened next is a mystery, but the next time Sinden was seen he had a wound to the head and was bleeding profusely. As he staggered back into the kitchen he was able to utter the words 'one blow did it' before collapsing. He lingered, unconscious, for four days before dying without regaining consciousness. He was hastily buried but his widow was, unsurprisingly, suspicious about his death and petitioned for his body to be disinterred and properly examined.

The eventual inquest was held at the Shaven Crown Inn. Sinden's widow claimed that Sir John has struck her husband in a drunken rage (an alternative suggestion was that he had pushed Sinden who had then struck his head on the fireplace) while Sir John maintained that the butler had simply fallen down the stairs on his way back to the kitchen that night. Other servants at Shipton Court testified that the butler had been entirely sober on the night of his death so was unlikely to have stumbled and fallen. Sir John's case had started to look rather weak until footman Joseph Wakefield appeared as a witness, claiming that Thomas Sinden had been constantly drunk for the entire week before his death and that, given his condition, it was quite likely that he had indeed tripped and fallen down the stairs. Since there were no witnesses to the moment when Sinden managed to acquire his injury (apart, perhaps, from Sir John of course) the case was closed as a 'natural death by the visitation of God'.

We will never know the true events leading up to the death of Thomas Sinden, but it is perhaps significant that Sir John Chandos Reade never again touched a drop of drink after the inquest. Furthermore, it seems that he changed his will shortly afterwards and on his death in 1868 it was discovered that he had disinherited his family and left his entire estate to a former footman by the name of Joseph Wakefield.

Whether Sir John continued to regret the accidental death of Thomas Sinden or whether he was forced to suffer for his murder in the afterlife is a moot point but his ghost haunted Shipton Court for many years. Eventually his presence became so bothersome that an exorcist was summoned and his spirit was walled up inside a hidden room. Presumably they had neither barrels nor ponds easily to hand.

The mention of ponds takes us back to Stanton Harcourt, the industrious poet Alexander Pope and not a ghost story but a curious case of either elemental excess or divine displeasure. During Pope's sojourn at the manor he became aware of John Hewett and Sarah Drew, a young couple who aimed to marry. It seems as if Oxfordshire was a pleasantly unprejudiced at the time as, in Pope's words: 'John was a well-set man, about five-and-twenty; Sarah a brown woman of eighteen … Their love was the talk, but not the scandal of the neighbourhood, for all they aimed at was the blameless possession of each other in marriage.'

Stanton Harcourt Manor

One afternoon in late July the couple were celebrating because John had just obtained permission to marry Sarah from her father. They were discussing wedding plans and John was weaving flowers for his fiancée's hair when an enormous thunderstorm rolled across the countryside sending all the farm workers scurrying for cover. The majority of the farm labourers headed inside but John and Sarah nestled themselves down into some hay piled high into a haystack. Lightning struck and thunder rolled. Sadly:

> The labourers, all solicitous for each other's safety, called to one another; those who were nearest our lovers, hearing no answer, stepped to the place where they lay. They first saw a little smoke, and after, this faithful pair John with one arm about Sarah's neck, and the other held over her face, as if to screen her from the lightning. They were dead. There was no mark or discolouring on their bodies, only that Sarah's eyebrow was a little singed, and a small spot between her breasts.

The tragic couple were buried together and Pope wrote an epitaph for their grave marker which included the lines

> Victims so pure heav'n saw well pleas'd
> And snatch'd them in celestial fire.

The marker plaque also stressed that they had been 'committed in marriage' because, almost immediately after their demise, local gossip began to question their purpose in the haystack and whether the bolt of lightning had been designed to prevent them celebrating their nuptials somewhat early ...

Pope wrote of the tragedy to Lady Mary Wortley[*] though hardly showing much empathy. 'The greatest honour people of this low degree could have was to be remembered on a little monument ...' He also produced another, unofficial, though very much more entertaining couplet about the event:

> *Here lie two poor lovers, who had the mishap*
> *Although very chaste people, to die of the Clap!*

---

[*] An unpleasant woman married to an equally nasty ex-ambassador to Turkey, a man who had been recalled to England because, according to Edith Sitwell, 'it was felt the Turks had suffered enough'.

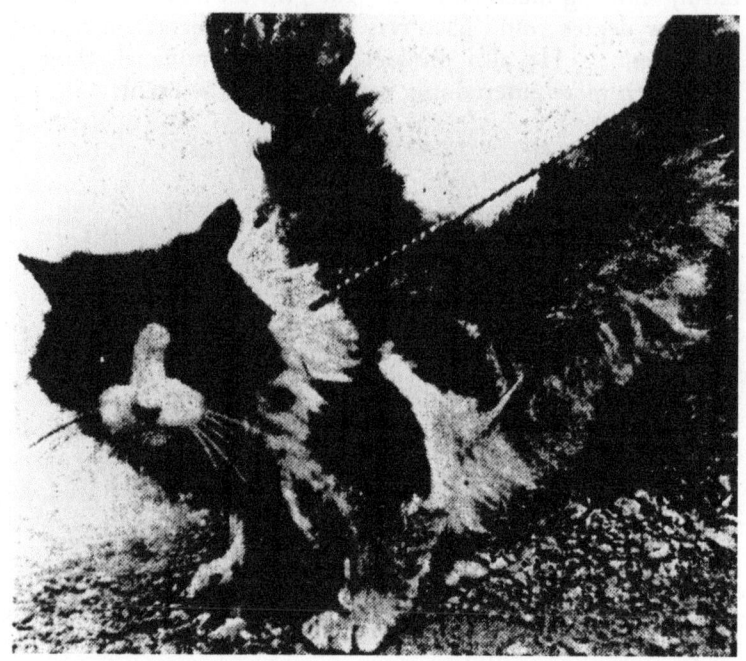

The winged cat of Oxford Zoo

Felix Aviatrix

LEAVING THE SUPERNATURAL for a moment let's move on to a rather different sort of cat story. On the evening of 9 June, 1933, Mrs. Hughes Griffiths of Summertown went out to check on the stables in her garden only to find that a black and white cat had somehow managed to worm its way into the building. As she approached the animal she was doubtless surprised when it unfurled a small pair of what looked like furry wings and leapt upwards towards one of the roof beams above her head. Mrs HG was adamant that the distance was 'considerable' and would have been too far for the animal to have jumped without some sort of assistance, and she described how it made rudimentary flapping motions with its wings as it jumped using them 'in a manner similar to that of a bird'.

Shocked at what she had seen Mrs HG called Oxford Zoo[*] who sent curator W. E. Sawyer and managing director Frank Owen to investigate. Luckily the two men had thought to bring along a net which they used to capture the cat; it subsequently found itself on display as an exhibit at the zoo. A reporter from the *Daily Mirror* wrote that he had 'carefully examined the cat tonight and there is no doubt about the wings, they grow just in front of its hindquarters.' The wings were reported to be around six inches long, but they do seem somewhat larger in the photograph. Unless of course it is a *very* small cat.

Reports of winged cats are not as rare as you might expect. A few years later in 1936 another winged cat was reported

---

[*] Which was actually based at Kidlington (on a site now occupied by the Thames Valley Police HQ building), making Oxford Zoo as accurate a description as Oxford London airport ...

at a farm near Portpatrick in Scotland, and 1939 a similar animal surfaced in Sheffield. There had also been previous reports from Cambridge in 1894 and Somerset in 1899. The generally accepted explanation is that the 'wings' are clumps of matted fur, an explanation which certainly held true for a celebrity moggie in West Virginia which was found one morning curled up in a box with two masses of fur beside it; the cat had shed its wings overnight. However, this is unlikely to be true in all cases. Both the Oxford and Sheffield cats were reportedly able to move their wings, indicating that they may have actually been part of the animals' bodies. There is a condition known as *feline cutaneous asthenia* (FCA) which causes extensive stretching of the skin around the shoulders of affected animals which might go some way towards explaining their strange appendages.

Lest you should think that this is a story firmly rooted in a less worldly past, we should note that winged cats were also reported from Russia in 2004 and China in 2008.

I made attempts to find out the fate of the fabulous flying feline but it seems to have been lost to history. Oxford Zoo closed in 1937 and many of the animals, along with all the zoo's records, were transferred to Dudley Zoo. Dudley Zoo is still in operation but they no longer have any records from Oxford. We can but hope that the cat lived out its days in comfort. And did not shed its wings.

It seems a shame to leave Oxford Zoo without mentioning the fact that among its attractions were three lions, two polar bears and an elephant called Rosie who played the mouth organ and who is now commemorated by a sculpture on a roundabout in the town. There were also three young Siberian wolves which managed to escape in January 1937 causing, understandably, considerable panic locally. One animal was quickly spotted in a garden near to the Northern Bypass. It tried to flee by jumping a fence but was shot and killed by Inspector Barnett, of Oxford police. The second was shot at Hampton Poyle later the same day, by a farmer who discovered it amongst his sheep.

The third wolf evaded capture for some time (during which time it managed to kill thirteen sheep) which means that I can justify including this story of a genuine Oxford where?

wolf.* A hunting party at Kidlington thought that they had killed the beast but were disappointed to discover that their trophy was a large dog. Eventually, after three days an *Oxford Mail* photographer of all people managed to bring the poor animal down at Harefield House in Summertown. I suppose we should be grateful that the zoo's lions were rather more securely caged.

---

* Sorry ...

The Hallelujah tree, Bicester

The Bicester Warlock

BICESTER IS DESCRIBED in the rhyme

Meat by the mile,
Beer by the pound,
When 'osses be okhard,
Turn 'em around.

– which refers to the meat market strung out along the old town shambles and the fact that horses would be broken in by being walked around a tree called the Hallelujah Tree near the town centre. The thought of a Hallelujah Tree is quite satisfying but Bicester does also have a story of supernatural interest to warrant our attention.

James Jagger was an illegitimate child who had been brought up in the Turnpike House* in Bicester by his guardian, George Gurden at the end of the eighteenth century. Gurden is described as a 'slipper, clog and pattin maker' and did his best to pass his skills on to his ward but it would seem that Jagger felt the life of a simple craftsman to be somewhat limiting and, to quote John Dunkin who documented the story in his 1826 *Anecdotes 2: Bicester*, 'this sedentary life led him, in moments of relaxation, to amuse himself with reading.' Sadly, this was long before the opening of Bicester public library and Jagger found the available reading matter limited to either the Bible or some books on heraldry. Luckily for him Bicester was the home of two savants who had previously published an astronomical almanac, their names being Dick Dodd and John Haines. Dodd managed to get himself into some kind of legal trouble and had to depart

---

* Sadly, now demolished.

Bicester in haste, but Haines was happy to take Jagger on as an unofficial apprentice[*] and the two studied astronomy, and of course astrology, together until Haines died in 1792.

Without the moderating influence of his mentor, it seems that Jagger's interests started to move away from the strictly scientific onto a more occult path and the following year he decided that he would attempt to summon the Devil himself! We will probably never know where he managed to acquire a grimoire with the correct spells and ceremonies to achieve such a thing, but somehow he managed to do so and set about his self-appointed task. And, amazingly, he succeeded. As his invocation proceeded a man-sized form, covered in shaggy black hair and possessing an impressive pair of horns appeared and attempted to seize him in a horrid embrace. Jagger immediately stopped his ritual and turned and fled in terror. Simultaneously the air was rent by the sound of a tremendous explosion which his confidants claimed was the sound of the Devil flying away across the rooftops, taking one of the chimney pots away with him.

It seems that the joke was on Jagger that day, because some of his 'friends', with whom he had shared his plans, had hatched a scheme to scare him. One had wrapped himself in a bull's hide and appeared as 'the Devil' and another had used gunpowder to create the supposedly demonic explosion. We might imagine that this rather public pranking would have dissuaded Jagger from further supernatural experimentation, and for a while it seems that it did, but he soon returned to his infernal invocations and, according to his own testimony at least, was soon able to summon minor demons to do his will whenever he wished. Certainly, from that point onwards, the people of the town said that Jagger had acquired the uncanny ability to detect thieves and recover lost property.

Because of his new reputation as a cunning man Mrs Saunders, landlady of the Rose and Crown[**] in Bicester, employed him to find a silver clasp which she had lost some time before. Arriving at the pub with due ceremony Jagger set out a bowl of water in the hallway and then moved to the room next door. Here he began to chant a spell which, he told

---

[*] According to Dunkin, Jagger had a day job as a barber.
[**] Now gone to the great brewery in the sky.

his audience, would enable him to recover the lost item. After some time he declared the invocation finished, and everyone present heard the unmistakable sound of a splash coming from the hallway. They returned to the bowl of water which, to the amazement of all, was found to contain the missing clasp.

Flushed with success, although according to some accounts inexplicably nervous as well, Jagger returned home to Turnpike House. Or at least he attempted to do so for, presumably in a fit of devilish retribution, just as he was about to enter the house he was swept up by an invisible force and whisked away across the rooftops of Coker Close. His previous nervousness had clearly been well-founded. Looking around him, Jagger saw that he was surrounded by 'numerous shapeless creatures, which, as they passed along, gradually assumed a form somewhat like asses, with panniers on their backs'. Gradually his abductors lowered the height of his headlong flight through the air until, by the time he reached the nearby King's End Field, he was low enough to be dragged through, at first trees and then bushes, hedges, ditches and even ponds. Eventually he was left, bedraggled and bleeding with his clothes half-torn from his body and covered in scratches in a field in Kirtlington Bottom, about four miles from Bicester. Here he remained, semi-conscious, half-naked and completely terrified all night until a group of farm labourers discovered him the following morning and escorted him home.

Unsurprisingly, this episode seems to have put paid to Jagger's ambitions to become a magician and the Warlock of Bicester fades into obscurity thereafter. It is always possible of course that his subsequent escapades were so successful that he managed to keep them entirely hidden from posterity.

Coker Close, Bicester

The deceptively calm waters of Black Jack's Hole

Tales from the Riverbank

WE COVERED A SERIES OF HAUNTINGS from the lanes around the county at the start of this book so let us now take a look at whether the Oxfordshire waterways are any safer to navigate. I'm tempted to suggest that they aren't ...

It is generally asserted that there has been an inn on the site of the Perch beside the river at Binsey for 800 years, but the present building can only be traced back to the 1600s. That said, it has had an unfortunately incendiary history in recent years having been extensively damaged by fires in 1957, 1977 and again in 2007.* The Perch used to be known as Binsey Cathedral – partly because of the casual approach of the then landlord to the Sunday opening hours legislation. Sited at the end of Binsey Lane (it is said that there are only two destinations to be found there: The Perch or the Church), it shares the village with the 'Treacle Well' made famous in Lewis Carroll's *Alice in Wonderland*. More properly called St Margaret's Well this was said to have been a healing well in mediaeval times and was especially famed for its ability to cure ocular difficulties.** St Margaret's Church has another unusual claim to fame: its very first Vicar was one Nicholas Brakespear who later went on to become the first (and only) English Pope. There is an interesting tradition associated with the church and well which maintains that if you have a problem or need an answer to a question you should drop a small stone into the well and mentally request a response. Then walk into the church and open the Bible on

---
* Presumably the fire alarms will be well-tested in 2047.
** Perhaps we should replace the village attractions with the pumps and the optics.

The view across to Port Meadow

the lectern; the first verse you see will give you the solution you require.

The pub has impressive literary credentials; Lewis Carroll performed his first public readings from Alice at the Perch (Alice herself later carved the image of St Frideswide on the church door), C. S. Lewis was a regular visitor, and the pub also featured regularly in the Inspector Morse novels. Even Dylan Thomas stopped by for a drink – although, on reflection, probably not just one. Furthermore, Gerard Manley Hopkins featured the trees outside in his poem *Binsey Poplars*: entirely retrospectively given that the poem was written to memorialise the riverside avenue being cut down. Fortunately, the trees have now been replanted.

But we are supposed to be discussing waterways. Just upriver of the Perch is a deep hole in the riverbed known as Black Jack's Hole (Anthony Wood refers to it as Black Jack's Pit) which was, to quote Stuart Fisher in *British River Navigations*, 'popular for suicides and catching pike'. This part of the river had such a dangerous reputation that parents would try to scare their children away from the spot by telling tales of a terrifying goblin who lived in a cave beneath the surface and who would leap out and drag them down to be consumed in his underwater lair.*

---

* It was not just young children who became Black Jack's victims – undergraduate Edward Schönberg died here in 1886 and Reginald Heslop drowned there aged 15, in 1890.

The Perch is said to be haunted by the ghost of a debt-ridden sailor who drowned himself at Black Jack's Hole and then returned to the pub after his death, where he is sometimes seen leaning against the bar with his arm outstretched as if reaching for a glass. On one occasion his appearance was rather more dramatic; drinkers told of a smartly dressed figure in a naval uniform who strode up to the bar, ordered a pint of beer and then promptly vanished before his order arrived. Other strange shadowy personages have also been reported although the histories behind these apparitions are unknown. Perhaps they are also drowning victims. Whatever their stories, they may not be local as their appearance is sometimes accompanied by the sound of voices speaking in an unknown (or at least unidentified) foreign tongue.

While not, perhaps, as memorable as 'Black Jack's Hole' there is a 'Bloomer's Hole' just upriver from Buscot Lock just by a rather splendid steel and wood single arch bridge. No-one is certain how it came by this name but there are two possible suggestions. One is that it is named after the local priest, the Rev. Bloomer, who was in the habit of swimming naked here, much to the disapproval of his parishioners; the other claims that the name commemorates a wagon driver named Bloomer who drove his horse and cart into the river at this point and drowned. This second explanation seems the more likely since his ghost, often along with his cart and unfortunate horse, is said to haunt the spot.

Unusually for Oxfordshire it is likely that the name of the village of Thrupp is derived from the old Norse, specifically from the Danish -fiorpe (-thorpe in modern terms), meaning 'village' and thus rendering any use of the phrase 'the village of Thrupp' redundant.* Local legend has it that the village was founded by a band of pillaging Vikings and the etymology of the name would seem to indicate that there was indeed some influx of Scandinavian settlers in the area at some point.** The village is recorded as Trop in the Domesday Book.

---

* I really should think these things through.
** A mass grave of Danes, probably killed during the St. Brice's Day Massacre of 1002, which was recently excavated in Oxford adds support to this argument.

Thrupp is nowadays mostly famous as a stop for recreational canal boats plying the Oxford Canal; the names of its two pubs, The Boat Inn and The Jolly Boatman (previously The Axe and The Britannia respectively) tending to confirm this slightly cruel assertion.

The pub names are doubtless a clue that both inns will have been pleased to see the canal construction pass by in the 1780s as the Irish construction workers, the Navigators or (of course) Navvies were notoriously heavy drinkers. The Boat Inn has a resident ghost, said to be that of a former customer who drank so much that he collapsed and died beside the bar; one can only wonder if he was one of those passing navvies. In any case he has remained at the pub and has been known to move objects around during the night and throw pots and pans from the kitchen shelves. On the anniversary of his death regulars used to swear that they would suddenly become aware of his 'distinctive aroma' making itself all too apparent in the bar. Allegedly anyway: no-one I spoke to could tell me the actual date of these olfactory occurrences.

Not all drowning victims come back to haunt pubs of course. The river passing beneath Burford Bridge, which is the southern half of the Thames crossing at the Nags Head Island in Abingdon, is haunted by a young woman who drowned there at some unspecified time in the past. Whether she fell into the river by accident or died by suicide by hurling herself from the bridge as some versions of the story assert is unknown. Witnesses have occasionally reported seeing her ghostly head and shoulders swept past the bridge although we can only assume that something makes it clear that she is a ghost since there is no record of a spate of emergency calls to the area.

Staying on the theme of emergencies, a gentleman by the name of Mr Thompson was cycling along the path between Iffley and Donnington Bridge back in 1963 when he spotted a boat which seemed to be in trouble. It was a dark evening and the vessel, which he described as being 'rather like the cabin cruisers which move up and down the river', was drifting silently in the current, clearly unpowered and askew to the flow. Despite dim lights being visible through the windows Mr Thompson described an eerie atmosphere surrounding the craft and experienced a weird frisson when he noticed a face

The Isis by Iffley Bridge – no phantom cruises apparent this evening

staring out at him from inside the cruiser. He dismounted from his bike and shouted across the river asking if he could do anything to assist; there was no reply, but he did notice a shadowy figure moving about on the deck. Resolving to go for help he climbed back onto his saddle and started off towards Oxford, giving one cursory glance back towards the mysterious boat. At which point he stopped in shock – not only had the cruiser completely disappeared but the surface of the river was unmistakably undisturbed. He cycled a little way up and down in an attempt to work out where the mysterious craft had gone but after a time, decided that this was a mystery he would never solve and continued into Oxford.

And a story, also from Oxford, from many years later; in this case it was told by Jenny and Jill, two young women taking a boating holiday sometime in the early 2000s. Having a day to spare they pulled over near the Osney Boatyard as the sun began to set, made themselves a meal and left their cruiser to head off into the town for an evening of all the best that Oxford had to offer. At some point, tired but happy, they returned to their boat and retired for the night.

The following day, perhaps understandably, they rose late and had an easy breakfast before heading back into Oxford to explore. At this point their recollections of the story vary somewhat. Jenny is certain that they came back to the boat for a late lunch whereas Jill insists that it was almost evening when they finally returned. In either case both women agree that they had something to eat and prepared to return to the city centre to round off their trip with an evening of partying.

As they sat companionably inside they were suddenly disturbed by the sound of shouting and splashing from outside. Jill dropped her book and Jenny struggled to open the door to see who was causing all this commotion. To their complete amazement they were entirely alone at their mooring, the river was silent and not a single ripple disturbed its surface.

Let's take a quick trip back just over a hundred years from their experience ...

Edgar George Wilson was a 21-year-old pharmacy assistant to William Luff who had a shop in Cornmarket. Edgar had a younger sister who was an aspiring musician so he left work on the lunchtime of 15 June 1889 to help her revise for an upcoming exam. Since he lived in West Oxford he decided to take the most direct route, along the river past Osney Mead, on his way back to work just after 2pm.

Christopher Green (9) and Thomas Hazell (10) had taken advantage of the same sunny afternoon to head off down to the river for a spot of light fishing. Neither boy was a strong swimmer and, being young boys, neither was taking very much care on the riverbank. Inevitably the worst happened and both boys ended up in the river, doubtless screaming for help. Luckily it was at that point that Edgar had reached their chosen spot near Boney's Bridge, a small footbridge just before the railway bridge across the river. Not even waiting to remove his heavy outer clothes, and despite not being a strong swimmer himself, Edgar leapt into the river to rescue the boys.

Reports of what happened next are somewhat confused. Whether he managed to help the boys to the bank or whether they managed to haul themselves out of the water isn't clear; what is certain is that Edgar, weighed down by his heavy clothing and quite possibly having become entangled in the boys' fishing lines, drowned while attempting to save them. Ironically, two other young men who were on the river in a rowboat and had also attempted to come to the boys' aid then

Boney's Bridge

tried to rescue Edgar, but his body had sunk below the surface before they managed to reach him. His body was recovered downstream some time later.

Edgar's heroic act clearly struck a chord in Oxford and an appeal led by the Oxford Young Men's Christian Organisation quickly raised £22 from over 2,000 local people to pay for a memorial which was placed beside the bridge in a ceremony attended by over 200 people on 7 November that year.

You can find the memorial, in the form of an engraved stone obelisk, beside the bridge today, just near the spot where the two girls moored up. Sometimes an entirely random encounter can lead to the unfolding of an intriguing mystery. I was told this story by Jenny some years later; neither she nor Jill had taken any notice of the memorial (it really wasn't that kind of holiday) so were unaware of the tragedy that had unfolded nearby over a century previously. But could they possibly have experienced a replay of the event? Or were the noises they heard the over-enthusiastic sounds of swimmers just out of sight around the bend, the sound clear in the still evening air? The two young women discussed the event at length over the next few days but could never entirely shake off the thought that they had experienced a genuine brush with the unexplained.

John Yeomans confronts a beast. Image published with permission of ProQuest. Further reproduction is prohibited without permission. Image produced by ProQuest as part of Early English Books Online. www.proquest.com

The North Aston Terror

AND SO TO ONE OF THE MOST detailed, yet least well known, of all the accounts in this book as described in a pamphlet printed in 1592 and written by one Edward White.* Under the snappy title of *'A true discourse of such strange and wonderful accidents as happened in the house of M. George Lee of North Aston in the county of Oxford, being in truth and a matter of such special weight and consequence as seldom hath the like been heard of before'* it details a series of phenomena experienced by a family living at a farm in North Aston.

The story began on 29 November, 1591, when George Lee started to experience 'diverse stones of contrary bigness' (anywhere between one and 22 pounds, that is up to 10 kilograms!) being violently flung into his home at North Aston. The stones rained down inside the farmhouse as if someone was crouched up in the rafters or as if they were passing directly through the roof or walls of the house. Despite the family searching for the source of the stones 'no man was able to conjecture whence they came saving they beheld them fall either through or the roof of the hall ... which caused the gentleman, his wife with his father and the rest of his friends to be greatly affrighted and terrified.' Despite the size and quantity of the stones falling no-one in the house was hurt.

Not knowing what else to do the family asked friends and neighbours to join them in an attempt to investigate these mysterious falls. Consequently, a sizable party duly arrived and congregated in one room, all except for a serving man named John Yeomans who remained in the main hall and squeezed

---

* With a pedigree like that how can it not be reliable?

Manor Farm, North Aston

himself into an alcove beside the fire saying he would keep watch from there. After around 45 minutes Yeomans was startled by noises coming from above his head and cried out in fear; when the rest of the household rushed to find out what was wrong they found another eight or nine stones on the floor.

Although this event was the last of that night the bombardment continued, off and on, throughout the next month. On the Feast of St Stephen (26 December) Lee invited his cousin Giles, who was the vicar of Aston, and various other neighbours to his house and they determined to play cards. An argument began over who should deal so Giles suggested pulling cards and whoever selected the first knave should be dealer. No sooner had he uttered these words than a large stone sailed across the room and smashed into the wall just above his shoulder. 'The first knave hath been dealt here indeed,' commented Giles – at which point another stone fell into the room and the men decided that perhaps praying would be a better use of their time than playing cards.

Even after numerous fervent bouts of prayer the assault of stones continued. Lee's sister Anne and her maid Joan who were staying the night at the house were subjected to a shower of stones while in the courtyard in front of the building. Moving indoors the deluge followed them until the servant John Yeomans called out to their tormentor 'If thou be a good fellow do us no harm, for we come not hither to do thee any'. The women and some of the men retreated into one of the bed chambers where two more stones fell, one of which struck a man named George Wright on the shoulder. Luckily, he was unhurt.

Later in the Christmas season two neighbours, William Whing and Richard Hickes, came to visit and were disappointed not to witness any mysterious events. Whing, emboldened by the calm, addressed whatever spirit was haunting the house saying 'Jack, if thou be a good fellow fling down a quoit or two that my companions and I may go and play at the quoits.' Almost immediately two ring-shaped stones were thrown towards the men. Surprised but not scared Whing asked for two more of the same and, sure enough, two similarly shaped stones promptly arrived. On examination, one of the stones was identified as having come from the green in front of the house; it was covered in grass stains and was recognisable as being a stone that the family had used on previous occasions.

Seeing that the mischievous sprite was now in a good mood, Hicks suggested that rather than produce more quoits it should show them something else and a large piece of mortar ('as if it had been pulled from some old wall') fell to the ground before them with sufficient force to break it into powder. This final fall persuaded the men that they should accept what they had been given; they proceeded outside and did indeed play quoits with the stones that 'Jack' had supplied.

The following night, as a small group gathered to keep watch, a clod of clay fell onto the nose of one of the serving maids who had fallen asleep. The maid cried out in shock, and no-one felt much like sleeping from that point onwards. As morning arrived Lee sent for the redoubtable John Yeomans (who lived at the other end of the village) and 'as he entered the little court before the hall he bespied a great black thing in the likeness of a dog, standing upright against the hall door as if it listened to what was done in the house'. Although initially terrified Yeomans, who is very much shaping up as the hero of the piece, shouted at the creature 'What are thou? In the name of God speak; if thou be a man speak or I will compel thee.' On receiving no reply Yeomans struck the beast repeatedly with his staff. The animal retreated to the corner of the courtyard, climbed upon a pile of stones and escaped over the garden wall.

Thinking that the excitement for the day was over, Lee sent Yeomans to check on a flock of sheep while he tried to get some much-needed sleep. The maid who had been woken during the night also attempted to rest on the floor of her master's chamber, but she was once again disturbed when a falling stone hit her on the shoulder. Moving to another position she was again struck by a stone and was horrified to see that the blaze in the fireplace began 'to flame very strangely ... suddenly very dark and dim [then] flaming forth into sundry changes of colour, but ever in the end it would be marvellous blue or marvellous black.' Terrified she retreated to huddle against the foot of the bed, only to witness the bedclothes pulled from the bed by an unseen hand.

Obviously this disturbed Lee from his slumbers – although whether he could have slept through the shockingly loud sound of footsteps which suddenly began echoing from the room above them is doubtful. Lee once again challenged the unseen presence but there was no response and he asked the maid if she would be willing to go and check the room upstairs.[*] On (doubtless somewhat nervously) entering the room the maid was stunned to see a naked sword, which had been sheathed and placed onto the bed the previous evening, thrust through the window and hanging from the sill by its hilt. The maid then took clothes down for Lee who dressed and came up to the room himself.[**]

As they examined the nearby rooms it was discovered that a number of bolsters had been thrown from one of the beds onto the floor. With remarkable foresight Lee called for a piece of chalk and carefully drew around their position before leaving the room; on his return the cushions were unmoved, but the chalk circle had disappeared. They re-marked the floor, left the room for 30 minutes and, once again, when they returned the lines had been erased. Determined not to be outdone Lee once again refreshed the chalk, but this time made the marks both thicker and wider. Again, they left the room and returned sometime later. This time the chalk marks remained; however, on the floor next to them was the unmistakable imprint of an animal's paw which was identified as being that of a young bear. Nearby was the clear imprint of a hawk's talon. These were not

---

[*] I bet John Yeomans would have gone himself.
[**] OK, that might pass as an excuse.

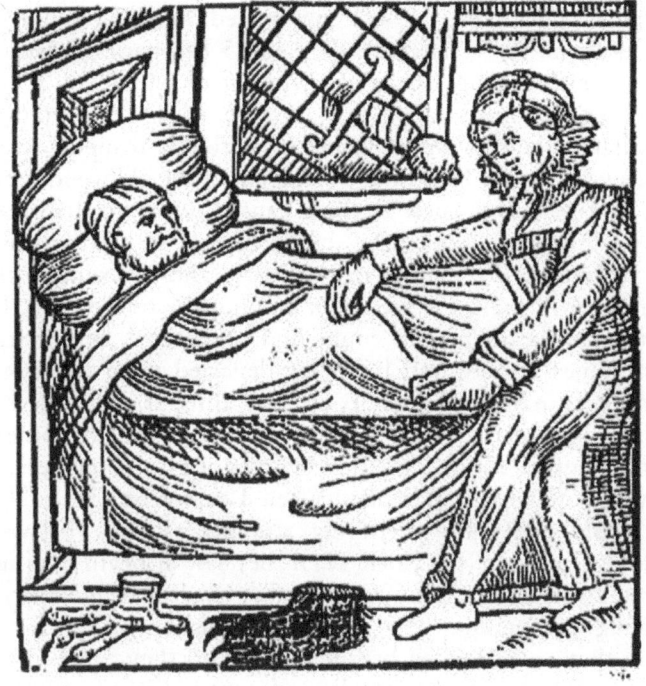

The Bear's paw and hawk's talon as depicted in the *True Discourse*.
Image published with permission of ProQuest. Further reproduction is
prohibited without permission. Image produced by ProQuest as part of Early
English Books Online. www.proquest.com

simple chalk prints; at the time of writing the pamphlet both marks were still visible in the wooden floorboard.

Later that day the same maid noticed a hare sitting beside one of the garden walls. It sat, unmoving, as she approached until she was within touching distance at which point it simply vanished before her eyes. Even after everything else that had happened Lee found it difficult to credit this tale – until he found a hare's footprint at the very spot the girl had observed the animal. When the animal was next spotted the family's spaniel dogs 'made more haste away from the hare than to follow her', which further strengthened the opinion that this was no ordinary animal.

After 6 January the fall of stones ceased, much to the joy of the household, but started up again on 15 February. In fact, in many ways things became worse with small puddles of blood an inch or two across appearing on the surface of the family dining table, puddles which would mysteriously reappear when wiped away as if the blood was oozing out of the old wood itself.

Obviously, events such as these caused widespread wonder and Sir Anthony Cope, the High Sheriff of Oxfordshire, came to interview everyone in the house and to examine the evidence for himself. He sent men up onto the roof to look for evidence of tampering but could find nothing to explain the fall of stones and he and his party departed none the wiser. A gentlemen named Thomas Power and three friends asked to stay the night at the farm in order to witness the phenomena and, they hoped, to solve the puzzle of its origins. They became somewhat offended and scoffed when Lee warned them that they would encounter 'terrifying strangeness', but 'between eleven and twelve of the clock, what they saw or heard I cannot tell, but their former boldness was now converted into fearful trembling and making what best they could out of the house I think they never looked behind them until they came to the parsonage where they knocked loudly until they were let in'. Not surprisingly, they refused to return to the farm.

One local man took one of the mysteriously appearing stones home with him but was almost immediately struck with excruciating pain in his eyes. He attributed this to having removed the object from the farm but, as the author points out, other stones were taken just as far away with no unfortunate consequences. Certainly, one visitor from Warwickshire who observed a stone fall directly in front of him and had Lee etch his name into the stone before taking it home as a souvenir, subsequently suffered no ill effects.

As if showers of stones and mysterious animal appearances were not enough of a trial, the pamphlet also mentions, almost as an afterthought, that the house was also plagued by blazing lights, 'sometimes such a light that the whole house was thought to be afire'.

There was one final, eerie, chapter to the story which reads like a scene from a horror film. Lee's wife (referred to only as Mistress Lee) sent a maid to the malting house one morning to check on the beer. The malting tub was covered in a blanket which the maid, to her horror, saw was moving around as if something was underneath it. Running to collect her mistress the two women returned and, somewhat nervously, pulled away the blanket only to observe 'an ugly black thing come creeping forth and falling to the ground [and] gliding along the floor to the door'. This creature was so horrifying that they were unable to offer any kind of description although, one of the workmen who came running on hearing their screams described it as being like a great black dog possessing the face of an ape but without legs or tail meaning that it wriggled across the floor on its belly. The creature retreated into a corner of the room but when those present summoned up the courage to approach they could find no trace of it, only the marks of its passing on the floor.

So, what could have been the cause of all this paranormal pandemonium? The author of the pamphlet is in no doubt. 'When Master George Lee was in the house then fell the stones with violent force and (as it were) followed him sometime. But in May last his life ended ... and since then nothing at all hath been heard or seen but all is as quiet as the heart can require'.

The case for the haunting being associated with Lee seems clear, but the agency behind the various phenomena must remain a mystery. All we can safely do is observe, once again, that perhaps sometimes it is people who are haunted ...

The strange creature from the maltings.
Image published with permission of ProQuest. Further reproduction is prohibited without permission.
Image produced by ProQuest as part of Early English Books Online.
www.proquest.com

The King Alfred's Head, Wantage

King Alfred's Head and Tales

AN OLD COACHING INN BUILT in the 1600s, the King Alfred's Head is set a little back from the main marketplace in Wantage allowing space for a small front courtyard away from the bustle of the town's through traffic. The pub cellars connect into a network of tunnels which, allegedly at least, criss-cross Wantage town centre linking many of the licenced hostelries together in a conspiracy of excise-dodging that supposedly dates back to the era of Georgian Black Wantage. This is difficult to confirm since most of the tunnels are now blocked off for safety reasons. In any case, the closer parts of these tunnels are used as beer cellars for the pub.

The current landlords, Michael and Katie, have experienced a number of odd, and sometimes inexplicable and frightening, experiences during their time at the pub and were kind enough to give me a guided tour of this fascinating building.

As you stand facing the door to the King Alfred's Head there is a window to the right behind which is a bedroom used by live-in staff and visiting guests alike. One previous chef regularly complained that he could not get a decent night's sleep when he used the room because of the constant sound of children running up and down the staircase outside the bedroom door; as you might expect there were no children living at the pub at the time. A family friend who also stayed here complained to his hosts that their cat had spent all night scratching at his door wanting to be let inside: he was somewhat perturbed to discover that the cat had spent the whole night shut in another bedroom...

Needless to say, the aforementioned subterranean storerooms are a favourite spot for odd activity. Katie described hearing

The network of tunnels under the pub. And under the town?

disembodied footsteps echoing along the tunnels when she worked alone in the area. One of the regulars at the pub had asked to see the cellars and was shocked to watch a crate of beer bottles shift abruptly to one side even though there was no-one nearby who could possibly have pushed it. Alana, one of the bar staff, often reported hearing unexplained sounds while working in the cellar and one night when she was downstairs bottling up she was startled by a loud crash, as if a crate of bottles or glasses had been thrown to the ground and smashed. Despite searching the area she could find nothing that might have been the source of the noise and there was no broken glass to be found. Shortly afterwards she described how an odd 'rushing breeze' swept past her in the dim light and at that point she decided that her tidying up could wait until the morning and she rushed back upstairs in fright. Becky, another employee, described being driven upstairs by the echo of voices emanating from the darkness at the far end of the cellar complex; she was further unnerved when the sound of unseen footsteps followed her up the stairs as she returned to the bar.

The unsafe nature of the tunnels demonstrated by the use of brick supports

Cobwebs and claustrophobia await unwary visitors

The gas meter is situated some distance into the tunnels, and it is perhaps unsurprising that the gas man never lingered long when the time to read it came around. Michael reported that when the flow of beer tails off in the bar the staff naturally assume that the barrel is empty; however when they venture downstairs to make the necessary changes to the supply they sometimes discover that the feed pipe has been physically pulled out from its connections. These fittings are very tight and it is very unlikely that they could come adrift of their own accord: there is clearly a mystery to be investigated here.

Other parts of the building seem to be similarly affected by these phenomena. Liam, the current chef, was working in the kitchen one evening when one of the fluorescent lights in the ceiling leapt from its mounting and struck him on the head. On investigation that fixing also seemed perfectly secure.

Upstairs there is a small function room which seats around a dozen guests and which overlooks the beer garden to the rear of the property. One summer evening Michael went to do some final clearing up in the room after an event and found the door locked and totally immovable. This might be construed as an accidental lockout except for one simple fact: there is no lock on the door – in fact there isn't even a latch mechanism behind the handle. Despite the best efforts of three members of staff the door remained immovable and they retreated in defeat resolving to attack the frame with heavy tools in the morning. When the morning came, they discovered that the door swung smoothly open when gently pushed. It is interesting to note that the family cat can often be found sitting outside this room staring through the door – but it can never be persuaded to cross the threshold.

I had high hopes for the attic of the pub and there are indeed two small rooms high up in the eaves. I asked if there had ever been any activity in these areas. 'The previous landlord told us never to go in there,' said Michael, 'so we never do'. Oh well, perhaps the floors are unsafe…

In any case mysterious voices can sometimes be heard coming from the upper floors and one past member of staff reported the sound of a crying baby. Curiously, she was expecting a baby herself at the time and no-one else she asked could hear anything untoward at all. Once her baby arrived she too ceased to be troubled by other-worldly wailing.

One evening a few years ago a young woman who described herself as a medium came into the King Alfred's for a drink and approached a member of staff to ask if they knew that their pub was haunted. Interested, the staff showed her around and she indicated that she could sense a woman with long hair in the large function room and, significantly, described small children playing on the staircase outside the guest bedroom. Down in the cellar she reported feeling many people passing in and out of the tunnel complex, although whether she meant that they were all present simultaneously or spread out over a long period of time is unclear. She also claimed that there was an entire phantom family in residence who were unhappy with all the changes which were occurring at the property.

This last remark is especially interesting. Michael had commented that activity in the pub coincided with either changes in staff or the times that the pub was either being redecorated or repaired. The last time the cellar walls were repainted all the fuses spontaneously blew, plunging the entire building into darkness; presumably not a pleasant experience for anyone down in the haunted tunnels.

Two significant events might serve to confirm that the ghostly family are indeed rather touchy. One Sunday evening, just after closing time, the pub was completely empty and Michael was alone behind the bar when he was astonished to see the heavy till fly from its position on the counter and crash to the floor. Thinking that someone had managed to get into the pub unseen he rushed out to look around but discovered that he was, as he had thought, the only person to hand. The till is surprisingly heavy and he struggled to get it back into position. Despite experimenting with some undignified pushing and shoving Michael was unable to easily move it around, especially since it had rubber feet designed specifically to stop it sliding when in use. Katie recently reported glimpsing a unknown figure moving around the bar although she was the only person present at the time. Similarly, barman Kieran reported seeing a shadowy apparition just recently in the same area. Could this figure be the mysterious till tipper?

The most interesting, and violent, event of all occurred shortly after Michael and Katie had returned to the pub after a spell working elsewhere. When they moved back into the Alfred's Head they decided to buy a new fridge which they subsequently installed in the kitchen of their upstairs flat. As well as the usual selection of food, milk and so on they stocked it with one large and two small plastic water bottles. Some days later, after enjoying a day out and about in the area, it was with both shock and surprise that the couple returned to the flat to discover a scene of some devastation, with the door of the new fridge blown open and food scattered across the floor in front of it. The water bottles had frozen solid and exploded, throwing open the door and scattering food across the kitchen. Or so they presumed. On investigation they discovered that the contents of the fridge door were entirely undamaged and although the larger bottle was indeed frozen solid and split apart the two smaller bottles were both still liquid, and also entirely intact. Even more strangely, plastic fridge magnets which had been attached to the outside of the fridge door were found snapped completely in two some distance away. Amazingly, the fridge was undamaged by this explosion and has worked flawlessly ever since. Thankfully, the incident was never repeated.

Michael and Katie are largely unfazed by all this paranormal activity and seem happy to remain at the pub, irrespective of with whom they are forced to share the property. Of course, sometimes Michael has to work away from home: 'It's a bit creepy then,' Katie confided.

At one point Katie and Michael briefly left the Alfred's Head which was, for a while, managed by Mike and Nikki. I called by to ask for an update on the situation and they admitted that they too had experienced the sound of footsteps running through the building and, on one occasion, awoke to find that the kettle in their upstairs kitchen had been mysteriously switched on. They also warned that the resident ghosts have taken to setting off the fire alarms whenever they are discussed at any length. I checked back the following week: sure enough, the fire alarm had gone off the day after my visit.

The cottage with the haunted chimney

Things That Go Bump in the Night

Finally, I trust you will forgive me if I finish with a more personal tale; something that might perhaps have had the potential to rival any of the previous stories had it continued. Back in the early 1990s a group of friends and I were asked to investigate a traditional country cottage which was experiencing some unusual events. The owners, Nick and his wife Kathy, had bought the property some five years previously in a somewhat dilapidated state with the intention of renovating it and restoring it to its previous glory, and they had succeeded admirably. The main part of the cottage was built around 1500 and was extended some five decades later to include the area which is now the kitchen space.

As part of their renovations Nick and Kathy opened up the original fireplace in the kitchen and lit a fire as an experiment; the outpouring of smoke alerted them to the fact that some serious remedial work was required and so they began exploring the chimney and fireplace area in earnest to determine the extent of any possible structural damage. The first thing they discovered was an iron rod wedged half-way up the chimney, placed so as to block access to the house from above. This was a common practice in earlier times, the belief being that the cold iron acted as a deterrent from witches and supernatural beings and offered a measure of protection from demons, goblins and the like, as well as more mundane intruders of course. Unworried by the threat of supernatural or mundane invasion they removed the obstruction and sealed the chimney in a more conventional manner with board. Furthermore, as they began to excavate behind the fireplace they discovered a collection of bones between the walls, which they identified as the remains of a cat which will have had been walled up as another ward. Note that the cat will probably have been a deceased pet 'repurposed' as a spiritual guardian after its natural demise: people weren't monsters in those days. In any case, the remains were hastily buried in the garden. As their excavations continued, they also discovered a bread oven which they delayed opening, possibly fearing what else they might discover. In the event the oven, once opened, turned out to be disappointingly empty.

Having cleared out the fireplace area a wood burning stove was fitted, along with a pipe up through the existing chimney. The iron rod was carefully propped inside the fireplace as a conversation piece and the whole of that part of the kitchen finished off with a fresh layer of plaster. The family had a holiday planned, so after all this work they metaphorically dusted off their hands and departed for pastures new, along with their three-year-old daughter, Holly. The plaster was just beginning to dry as they left the house.

On their return a week later they were surprised, if not amazed, to discover an odd indentation at around ankle height in their new plaster beside the base of the wood burner; on closer examination it seemed like an unnaturally elongated handprint. Now, no-one had keys to the house and there were no signs of a break-in, nor was anything missing, so who had made the mark? The print was perfectly formed with the twin moons of the heel of a hand clearly visible and long curved marks from the fingers which tapered almost to claws. The thumb was scarcely visible but could be felt as an indentation; its position indicated that it was a left hand that made the marks. The print measured 9cm (3.5 inches) across but was an abnormally long 22cm (8.5

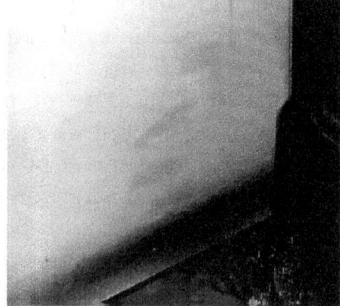

The mysterious hand print at
the base of the woodburner

inches) from base to fingertip. Experiments failed to replicate such an accurate shape by dragging the fingers in an attempt at elongation. In any case who could have been in the cottage to make the impression?

Photographs taken at the time do not do justice to the imprint, but they do give some feel for the eerie quality of the mark.

Perhaps Nick and Kathy should have taken notice of the previous owners; when they bought the cottage they had been asked if they were afraid of ghosts. After their discovery they were understandably disturbed, especially when they began to hear noises at night coming from the kitchen. When they cautiously investigated there was nothing untoward to be seen, certainly nothing to match up to the sounds they had been hearing. But the noises continued nonetheless.

As if that wasn't disturbing enough young Holly started seemingly watching someone move around the house and sometimes laughed as if at an unheard remark – but most children do that. Don't they? Footsteps began to echo around the kitchen and up the stairs at night and wind chimes kept indoors would ring softly to themselves on balmy nights. But surely these are easily explainable: aren't all old houses draughty and don't they settle and creak when they cool?

The couple originally treated their experiences as something of a joke (although neither of them expressed a particular desire to go down to the kitchen after dark) but gradually the night-time noise and Holly's increasingly disturbing behaviour led to family tension; eventually they decided to ask for help and, through a friend, contacted a local paranormal investigation group.

It was hardly a thorough investigation since Nick and Kathy were, understandably perhaps, just eager to return their lives to normal and the most obvious solution seemed to be to put back the iron barrier which had, arguably anyway, been the catalyst for the whole episode.* The couple were certainly happy to give this a try to see if it helped. The rod was consequently restored, if not to its original position then at least back in the chimney, and they went to bed that night hoping that their haunting was over.

---

* They were understandably reluctant to exhume the cat.

And, much to everyone's surprise, it proved to be so. Whether it was the simple psychological closure of returning the rod to the chimney which ended their haunting or whether removing it had actually unleashed a boggart or other supernatural nuisance which was now once again securely excluded is a subject for a long discussion, but the family were much relieved that their ordeal was over. Nick was undecided on which explanation to believe, but he did resolve to leave the rod in place and quickly plastered over the mysterious handprint. He also decided that, should they ever sell the house, he would be sure to ask the new owners if they believed in ghosts ...

Epilogue

AND THERE WE MUST LEAVE the weird phenomena of Oxfordshire: I hope you have found something to entertain you; something to evoke a minor frisson of fear perhaps; but, most of all, something to make you pause and reflect. I have deliberately taken an agnostic approach to all these stories because, in the end, they are just that: stories. But all stories grow from a tiny seed of truth, the fun is in extracting the kernel of the matter from the chaff of the tale. It really doesn't matter whether or not you believe in ghosts, UFOs or strange animals roaming the countryside, I just hope you agree that the thrill of the chase is as interesting as any possible resolution and that sometimes, just sometimes, there are things which are better left a mystery. So, with ghosts in mind and whether you are reading this during the day or late at night, let me leave you with a few lines from Henry Wadsworth Longfellow to ponder before you go:

> All houses wherein men have lived and died
> Are haunted houses. Through the open doors
> The harmless phantoms in their errands glide,
> With feet that make no sound upon the floors ...

Sweet dreams.